Black Hole Blues

Praise for Patrick Wensink

"Deliciously dark and funny."
– LOUISVILLE-COURIER JOURNAL

"This is Wensink's special touch: to go as far out as possible with character and concept, but still drive a deeper meaning home. He does so by mixing his Palahniukian style with the kind of twisted humor you can normally only find on Adult Swim." – LEO WEEKLY

"In Wensink's world 'nothing special' always turns 'mucho weirdo' before the story is over." – PANK

"One of those rare gifts we get every now and again."
– THE FANZINE

"Irreverent, outrageous, and fearless in his choice of material, Patrick Wensink has a true knack for absurdity."
– JOEY GOEBEL, author of *Torture the Artist*

"In his collection of stories Sex Dungeon For Sale!, Patrick Wensink demonstrates a gift for darkly absurdist humor that (just guessing here) surely derives from watching either too much or not enough television."
– JAMES GREER, author of *Artificial Light* and *The Failure*

"Absurd, surreal, and funny." – LANCE CARBUNCLE, author of *Smashed, Squashed, Splattered, Chewed, Chunked, and Spewed*

"Wensink has a sharp wit on display."
– JORDAN KRALL, author of *Fistful of Feet*

Black Hole Blues

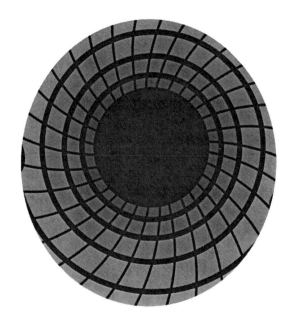

Patrick Wensink

LAZY FASCIST PRESS
PORTLAND, OREGON

LAZY FASCIST PRESS

AN IMPRINT OF ERASERHEAD PRESS

830 NE BRYANT STREET
PORTLAND, OR 9211

WWW.ERASERHEADPRESS.COM

ISBN: 1-936383-51-9

Printed in the USA.

Thank you:

The Boss
Little Billy Ocean
Matt Dobson
Cameron Pierce
Carlton Mellick III
Rose O'Keefe
Jason Jordan
Lauren Becker
Kevin Donihe

ONE

"There's no sacrifice too great for a shot at immortality."
   -J. Claude Caruthers, *Nashville's Shakespeare*[1]

Someone once said: "Being a genius is a real shot in the nuts. Shit's exhausting as all hell."

That someone was country music legend J. Claude Caruthers.

When said philosophical nugget was scratched into his autobiography, *Nashville's Shakespeare*, Caruthers had no idea how true it was. He just thought it sounded cool.

Recently, that genius swallowed every ounce of the singer's energy until he was a sleepwalking shell of a man. The exhaustion was so powerful, so numbing, he barely noticed Judy yanking off his scruffy boot.

See, Claude hadn't slept for more than a week because that genius was currently suffocating beneath the greatest artistic achievement in Nashville history. Well, at least since Willie Nelson sculpted a Venus de Milo from rolling papers soaked in Coors beer.

When that boot finally slipped free, J. Claude's tour bus was pounding down the road. Nighttime highway lights peeked through crushed velvet curtains and disappeared across the carpet. The singer's bedroom occupied the cruiser's rear and was draped from ceiling to floor in purple. It'd been nearly

---

1 Upon further research, the author discovered this was actually first spoken by Humphrey Bogart in the 1950 film, In a Lonely Place.

thirty years since the quarters were redecorated and they had barely been cleaned during that span.

Judy popped off the boot and fell backward onto Claude's bed. The publicist, several decades younger than the wrinkled star, was a leggy dream with soft red hair now spread across the pillow. This was a treat since her locks were normally twisted up like a tight coil of copper wire. J. Claude oozed a long glance at her tiny feet, thin ankles and girlishly small hands. The five-time Country Musician of the Year made a big show of licking his lips.

Claude's black sideburns were fading grey and his bones ached. But the songster didn't notice when his heart got to beating like that. He assumed the handsomeness discussed in *Nashville's Shakespeare*—rugged good looks that made the Marlboro Man feel "downright gay"—were responsible for Judy's seductive tumble. His mind's green lights flashed to crank up that famed Caruthers Charm.

Even though the exhausted flesh around them was puffy and discolored from insomnia, his eyes managed to sparkle with jumping jacks of trouble. "Take off your dress," he said. "Stay a while."

"No, thanks, my dress is fine," she glowered and stood, finding sea legs as the bus swayed. Judy swept crumbs and cigarette ash from that blue cotton dress with a sigh. "Some days, Claude, you are like gum in my hair." She tossed the boot in his direction.

"Oooh, that sounds kinky. I could get into that."

Purple braided ceiling tassels, coated in three decades of nicotine, beat into the publicist's head. Her stomach tensed. When J. Claude's eggplant bedspread, violet wallpaper and lilac carpet mixed with the bus' motion, she still ached with nausea, even after all these years.

Judy wanted to deliver a Hall of Fame scowl. She wanted to make Claude cry.

Instead, she settled for her natural reaction of pity, marveling at her boss' face, weathered by decades of smoky clubs and all-night gigs. "You have an interview. His name is Martin Dobson. He's riding along until we get to Nashville. I'm going to patch him over to you." She pointed at the dilapidated intercom system that was pretty hot shit back when the bus was new.

"Aw, relax," J. Claude hopped down from the window seat. His strut was cracked and dry with beef jerky stiffness. His every movement was a faded copy of its once suave self. "Sit back down on the bed. Let's me and you have a one-on-one business meeting first."

The singer eyed a pinpoint scar on her nose: the telling remains of a long-removed piercing. Caruthers wondered once again if it was a diamond stud, a cute little hoop or a chrome ball. Who knew, because the carefree girl who once fit behind a nose ring was long gone. In her place was a woman strict with schedules, marketing agendas and *Billboard* chart figures.

Her only carefree moments were spent attached to a coffee cup. Strong, black java left a flavor in her mouth. She loved that taste.

"How about you act like a decent human being and let Mr. Dobson into your lair?" Judy's face bunched and her arm made a dramatic swoop.

Claude's bright green eyes lit with possibility, the way they always did upon discovering yet another distraction from life's work. "I put the lay in lair, if you know what I—"

"Claude," she clapped her hands for attention.

A shocked trail of cigarette smoke slithered from his lips.

"It'd be good for publicity if you spoke man-to-man." She snatched a thermal coffee mug off a shelf and drank. Closed eyes. And breathed.

The guitar strummer painfully thumped onto the mattress. A skeleton of springs showed through the bed. He propped himself against a wood-paneled wall where several holes had been patched with dull silver tape.

"No time," he lifted Rusty from the floor and plucked a sour G chord. It seemed his guitar could never make up its mind about staying in tune, constantly wobbling back and forth.

Rusty, J. Claude's maple acoustic, had seen better days. Caruthers refused to have any crew member so much as change a string since the Alice-to-Gwendolyn tour of the early 80s. Three decades of spilled beer, honky-tonk smoke and filthy finger picking covered the instrument in a thin layer of tar. "Now Judy, maybe you're one of those mentally retarded kids I donate so much money to, but if not, you should know I'm writing the most important damn song of my life here. Probably the most important song the world's ever known. Silent Night, Ground Control to Major Tom, Footloose, they're nothing compared to this and you know it. Quit trying to distract me."

"Those kids aren't retarded, they're orphans. And you've been writing one song for three years," her voice was bored, tired of arguing this fact every day. "And I really doubt it's more important than Silent Night." She shook her head and in a deep grumble whispered: "Probably not even Footloose."

Claude offered the grungy guitar to Judy. "You want to try and be Nashville's Shakespeare?" He tipped back his cowboy hat as if he and the redhead were nearing a gunfight. The hat carried as much gunk as the guitar and its snakeskin band was shredded. Caruthers was careful not to tip things too far and expose his bald spot.

Judy popped a shallow laugh. "Nobody calls you Shakespeare but you." She swayed with the bus' movements and waited for an answer.

"Somebody must, I mean it's airbrushed on the side of the damn bus."

Her eyes rolled and she shifted shoulder blades. Caruthers kept the room hot and the dress clung to her moist skin.

Judy took another relaxing breath and a quick coffee sip,

reminding herself this was the life she'd chosen. There probably were better publicity jobs out there, but something kept her on board. Maybe it was when Claude showed frequent glimmers of innocence, those little dashes of sweetness once in a while. Or maybe it was because his artistic powers were still carved from granite. Love him or hate him, Claude was fun to watch up on stage.

But, still fuming, Judy asked for the millionth time how this was better than a corner office with Daddy's firm? She couldn't help but laugh at this mess.

Claude's attention went back to the fretboard. "Wipe that smirk off your face before I wipe it off with a silver Colt." Claude plucked the acoustic's fattest string with one hand and torqued its tuning peg with the other.

"Boss, I wasn't smiling," Judy said with a pair of flat, unhappy lips.

J. Claude wished she had smiled. The only truth in his autobiography was a passion for making people smile. Especially ladies. Judy seemed like the one woman he couldn't crack.

"Plus, the judge took away your gun license. Took away your stupid arsenal, too. Remember?"

He strummed a chord and sniffed at the bacon frying in the bus' tiny kitchen. "Well, call old mister black robe and sign me up for one of those special twenty-four hour gun licenses."

There was a beat where Judy squinted at the star. He returned the look.

"Let me get this straight, you want me to acquire a gun license that doesn't even exist, so you can shoot me?" Judy steadied herself against the wall, the bus lights flickered. "Again?"

"What? Am I on trial? You can't take me to court twice. That's double jeopardy. Plus, the shooting was an accident. How was I supposed to know you'd be walking past my target?"

"You set up your target in front of my motel room." Her forehead and cheeks were red as her hair. A thick vein crawled up her neck. "That's your idea of an accident?"

"Bing—" he picked Rusty's string. "Bing—" he cleared his throat. Nashville's Shakespeare plucked it again and sang with golden vocal cords: "Biiiiiiiiiingo."

It pained Judy to admit it, but J. Claude's voice still sounded good. It still made steel workers cry and grandmothers turn their panties into white cotton rain storms over the stage.

Those pipes were, however, not a secret to J. Claude.

Nashville's Shakespeare dissected various elements that created a singing voice so pure and perfect Caruthers once dreamt God requested the country legend sing Heaven's national anthem. According to the biography, the Big Man Upstairs proclaimed J. Claude's pipes to be his greatest invention—better than catfish, chewing tobacco and deer hunting, combined. Rumor, or just Nashville's Shakespeare, claimed Kenny Rogers was still burned up about that one, since Rogers assumed his vocals were superior. The book went to great lengths to sprinkle gasoline and lit matches over their rivalry. One chapter, titled, "Seventy-Eight Reasons Kenny Rogers is a Pussy," included illustrations of the snow-bearded Texan wearing a dress and sucking his thumb.

"I'll get right on the phone with Judge Tompkins." Judy opened the curtain and watched midnight lights flash past. "For now, put down Rusty and talk to this reporter before another writer, with publicity you desperately need after Missoula, runs off and prints something nasty."

"Yeah, yeah, yeah," Claude's voice evaporated as he squinted at the guitar. A familiar cramp found his belly—the same one that stabbed whenever J. Claude privately begged the filthy guitar for help.

That ugly feeling started back in 1977. It was once an inkspot, a dash of pepper, a nasty speck of blackness in his belly where people normally get tickles of joy and happiness. But that tiny punctuation mark of dread grew with each song he wrote, until it swallowed him whole.

"Yeah, yeah, yeah." J. Claude took a comforting breath, knowing he only had one more song to write before he did something awful to end these black feelings.

TWO

"A lot of folks ask me who'd win in a fight between myself and Charles Lindbergh. And I'm always like, 'huh?' My fans like to drink a little bit, you know."
  -J. Claude Caruthers, *Nashville's Shakespeare*

"Karen, we don't complain. We're scientists," J. Claude's brother, Lloyd, proudly told the young laboratory assistant. He patted her hand with care and saw the woman's anger disappear. Nothing made Lloyd Caruthers happier than teaching. Nothing except maybe an evening watching his favorite movie, The Gambler Returns, or maybe listening to Kenny Rogers and Dolly Parton's duets album.

"You're right." She twisted a shiny silver ring on her hand. "The Hadron Collider is more important than my feelings." Karen removed thick glasses from a lab coat pocket. "So what if we don't get to be the first team to test it? We'll eventually run our research, right? Just not as soon as those Team Orange assholes." Her eyes bulged and she covered her mouth in apology.

Lloyd, the senior member of an astrophysical research team, gave Karen a confident face and a wink, like she'd just uncorked the secret to his well-documented scientific success. She was young, but catching on impressively fast.

"It's alright, Karen," Lloyd said in that voice. Unlike Claude—whose southern inflections seemed to wind tighter every passing year—a few decades abroad gave Lloyd's speech a soft, international flair.

Accents weren't the only thing separating them. Lloyd Caruthers was about as different from his brother as a bottle of Coke from a Molotov cocktail. Where Nashville's Shakespeare looked like he existed on a diet of water and Camel Lights, the brilliant twin carried soft bulk in his stomach from a steady stream of sausage and dumplings. Claude was a man of the people, while Lloyd hid from the world, deep inside a cocoon called physics. So deep, he worked in a lab far underground. Unlike Claude, Lloyd held three doctorate degrees, wore a ponytail and hated country music. Except, of course, for Kenny Rogers' velvet voice.

Karen was Lloyd's heir apparent in every way, except her bouncy cheer. A determined physicist, Lloyd concluded decades earlier, must be focused. He must wipe all joy and excitement from the job, sanitize it until nothing remains but brutal clean fact. Caruthers hoped this misery and sacrifice would stand as a legacy future generations could admire.

Lloyd looked around the room, but his current legacy spelled nothing but disappointment. None of the computer screens spinning with data and bar charts was going to beat Team Orange. The tidy room's small window showed hard-hatted men ratcheting together the finishing touches on the Hadron Collider—the culmination of his life's work. While most would have filled with pride at its sight, a guillotine chopped any enjoyment from Lloyd's job, knowing Team Orange beat him to the punch.

"Nobody can name the second man in space," he often snickered when his work ethic dissolved. After twenty-four hour research binges, he often needed brutal encouragement to continue. "Nobody knows who flew the second plane across the ocean after Lindbergh."

Lloyd's chest twisted into a disgusted knot at the realization he would soon become the number-two man in space, Gherman Titov, and Charles A. Levine, the silver medalist in the great Atlantic race, all rolled into one.

A psychiatrist once said Lloyd needed to stop torturing himself with these thoughts. His numerous ulcers were now bleeding and the stress was like shaking salt over these internal lesions. "And don't even get me started on your hand pain," that doctor once snapped.

But, for professionalism's sake, Lloyd bottled up this disappointment for another day. "Mmmmmmmmhhhhphh," that voice was hollow. The physicist's hand tingled whenever he lied like this. "Karen, it's a good challenge for our team to work harder and prove that our research is more important to physics than Team Orange's. We'll leave our mark a little bolder in the history books when the atoms settle. Trust me."

The atoms were scheduled to settle soon.

Lloyd and Team Green were dozens of meters below the Swiss and French border, working on the most advanced physics project in history. The Hadron Collider was an underground seventeen mile circular concrete track intent on recreating the Big Bang. It didn't look much like a track, though. It was a thick insulated pipe with rainbows of wire spiraling around it. Two protons would soon be fired through each side of the circular tube, blazing a hair under the speed of light, until they smashed into one another. The entire project required as much electricity as nearby Geneva.

Over six billion Euro and nearly fifteen years went into building, testing and theorizing over those two microscopic particles and the possible results when the atoms settled. They were easily the most important protons in history. Scientists claimed this mini-Big Bang would mark immeasurable advances in physics and better explain the creation of the universe.

Doomsday prophets, on the other hand, believed a much blacker idea of what might occur.

"I should look to you for more inspiration, Doctor Caruthers." Karen gazed into her boss' eyes. "You could complain about our Team being passed over, but you don't. You could complain about our lack of funding, but you don't. You could complain about your hand, but you don't. You're a rock, sir—"

"Thank you, Karen," his face turned red and wet. Lloyd rested a palm on his hefty stomach and stared up at the popping, crackling fluorescent bulbs. This went on until his embarrassment took a nap.

"Yeah, doc," a familiar voice called from the corner of the lab.

The scent of lemon cleaner stung Lloyd and made a headache. It wasn't allergies, but the realization that Veronique, the janitor, was listening. The astrophysicist fantasized about someday introducing her as Mrs. Lloyd Caruthers and the last thing he wanted to discuss was that stupid, stupid hand.

"What is with the rubber fingers?" Veronique said, smiling in her blue worker's jumpsuit and holding a mop. Her blonde Swiss hair was practically the same white as the walls. She moved with a graceful sway that begged Lloyd to wrap arms around her.

Droplets of grey mop water hit the floor and puddled during the silence.

"My h-hand?" Lloyd said a little prayer that maybe a comet would destroy the lab so he wouldn't have to answer. "Mmm-mmmmhhhhphh."

"The prosthetic hand, right there," Veronique said in that cute accent. She leaned her weight on the mop.

"Oh, this?" he twisted the wrist to show both sides of a motionless doll flesh appendage. He cleared a nervous throat and mumbled: "Science took it."

"Oh." Veronique blushed.

"Oh." Karen's eyes grew large again.

After a few minutes of uncomfortable paper shuffling and floor swabbing, both women left the doctor alone with his mementos of failure. Being a glutton for punishment, Lloyd reached into his desk for the worst penalty imaginable.

He lined up a jury of three framed pictures and paced the flour white floor. He hoped the photos' judgment would help him forget stumbled opportunities with Veronique. He also secretly hoped they'd inspire a plan to leapfrog Team Orange.

"Einstein," he said to the famous pose of Albert Einstein with his tongue out. "You jerk. I bet I'm taller than you." He wasn't, Mr. $E=MC^2$ was five-nine. The Caruthers twins only reached five-four-and-a-half, at best.

Oddly, Lloyd's self-esteem did rise.

"Robert," he told the photo of a dashing Robert Oppenheimer, the father of the atomic bomb. "I don't hate you like these other assholes, but damn it, I need some help here."

The lab machines beeped and the computer charts rose and fell as erratically as Lloyd's self-opinion.

"And you," he sneered at his closest competition, a wheelchair-bound Stephen Hawking. "You'll be a footnote in physics when I'm done." He squinted hard into the British scientist's face as if a knife fight were breaking out. Lloyd, unfortunately, couldn't intimidate a block of cheese and said the meanest thing imaginable: "I hope you get food poisoning."

A tiny hiccup.

A silent gasp.

A frigid swallowed breath gave Lloyd a jolt.

Greek weddings broke out in his mind, plates of thought shattered within his skull and an idea opened amongst the mess. It was so small Lloyd didn't notice at first. But soon, the answer to all his problems spread wider and claimed more real estate in his brain until it couldn't be stopped.

Lloyd was reminded of a strange letter he recently opened. The subject of the note was, oddly, food poisoning.

THREE

"Oh, hell yes, the Ladies' Project's about all the girls I rocked in the sack."

   -J. Claude Caruthers, *Nashville's Shakespeare*

"Wow, wow," the kid reporter said, walking into the bus' plum-colored bedroom, wearing wrinkled jeans and a t-shirt. He inhaled stale smoke and grinned with every tooth. "Big fan, sir. Wow. My mom's name is Michelle, so, uh, you know. You mean a lot to us."

"Ah, yes," J. Claude said from the high stool that made him feel taller. Without hesitation he was strumming Rusty and singing a ballad:

Oh, Michelle, Michelle
I don't wanna run off to the chapel
Oh, Michelle, Michelle
'Cause if we get married
You'll get plump as an apple

"If I had ears, I'd stab them right now," Rusty, the guitar, thought. "Stop clapping kid, don't encourage him. Please, Claude, wipe that look off your face."

Rusty couldn't see J. Claude's face, but knew the singer wore an enormous smile, stooping so low again.

"The old J. Claude Caruthers wouldn't do this bullshit," the guitar thought, remembering their glory days in the seventies.

The days when he and Caruthers filled stadiums. Back when their music meant something. Back when every guitar in the equipment van wanted to suck Rusty's dick. "We never had to do this song and dance for anyone, buddy," he silently pleaded. "The song and dance came to us."

Rusty's strings slipped gently out of tune, hoping J. Claude would save some dignity and shut his mouth. To the guitar's shock, his owner played the entire song. It took five excruciating minutes.

J. Claude fielded a request to sing that tune None Sweeta than Rita and Martin Dobson, the interviewer, turned pink with joy. Rusty could tell from the peppy chord changes that J. Claude loved making people happy. Rusty used to enjoy making smiles too, back before writing songs turned into punching a time clock.

"Do you mind if I record our chat?" Dobson asked, pulling out a small black tape recorder.

"Hey, that's the same model I use for song ideas. Record away."

"Really? The LR six-thousand or the LR seven-thousand?"

There was a silent note of confusion. "Beats the hell out of me. Always sounds like I'm singing through a toilet, either way."

"Oh, right, well, still very cool." Dobson cleared his throat. "Tell me, mister Caruthers, what are you most proud of in your career?" the kid said, clamping his enormous teeth on a pen and settling into one of the shorter chairs.

The singer rubbed fingertips together. They were stiff and thick, callused from years of playing. Claude loved the hard, dead skin on his fingers. He wore them as a status symbol of decades on the road.

"Please, call me J. Claude, or hell, we're friends right?" the multiple Grammy winner gave an aw shucks voice. "Just call me Jay. Cigarette?"

"Oh, I gave it up…but just this once." To Rusty, the kid's smooth face wasn't old enough to actually buy a pack of smokes. "I mean, sharing a smoke with Nashville's Shakespeare, wow. Thanks, Jay."

Rusty didn't know whether to be depressed or enraged. "Oh, Claude, nobody calls you Jay and nobody calls you Nashville's Shakespeare. Man, just be yourself. You haven't been yourself since Stella died."

If Rusty had eyes, they would have been crying with Claude's gentle strumming. His owner dug deeper into the persona of J. Claude Caruthers. A pain Rusty could only compare to someone peeling off his thin maple planks, skinning him alive, overcame the guitar.

"Look at him. Shit, look at us," the guitar thought. "What makes a man turn his back on himself like this?"

"Now, where were we?" J. Claude said as thick plumes of tobacco stink filled Rusty's open body. "My proudest achievement? Well, it'd have to be the two-thousand-one-hundred-thirty-three songs I've recorded so far for The Ladies' Project, as Rusty and I call it." He smacked his best friend like a bongo.

"Your autobiography says the project is, in alphabetical order, one love song for every female you've ever slept with, correct?" the kid casually pointed the orange cigarette tip in J. Claude's direction. "By the way, loved the book. Pure genius."

"Aw, thank you. But, nah," J. Claude's laugh made the guitar tremble. Rusty knew what was coming. "I've bagged a lot of tail in my time. No doubt." Caruthers gave a soft, arcing whistle. "Maybe even more than a couple thousand, but the project is simply based on every woman's name in the dictionary, not the many, many," he coughed, "many girls I've rocked in bed. Rusty and I have written about them all, well practically all."

"Not again," the guitar thought. "Claude, you know that's not true. You know you're too scared or depressed or something to even touch another woman."

"Our readers are curious, Jay, when will you finish The Ladies' Project?"

"Oh, shucks. I probably shouldn't…"

"Please…"

"Mercy! Uncle!" Claude delivered a twenty-four karat laugh. "You win." The bus hit the brakes and both men shifted violently. "Tomorrow night, actually. I'll be debuting my last song at the Country Music Awards."

"Really? We've heard you've been trying to finish for years." The kid ran fingers over the purple drapery. He kicked at the hardened remains of a sandwich on the floor.

"I'm taking my time, son. I got one song left. Rusty and I have been whittling away all the rough edges until it's tender and perfect as a lady's thigh. If you'd have dedicated thirty years of your life to writing songs, you'd make damn sure the last one was a winner too."

Rusty sensed something in J. Claude's voice whenever he talked about the song. The guitar knew Caruthers had some ugly master plan for the finale, but didn't know what.

"What's her name?" Dobson's voice was a snake hypnotized from its basket by a professional charmer.

J. Claude's golden throat made nervous little hums, like the name gave him heartburn. "Zygmut." He sighed. "It's Polish, means Radish Soup or Dirty Diaper or some such nonsense."

"Wow, sounds like a challenge."

The guitar noticed J. Claude's entire body stiffen. "I won't lie to you, some days rhyming words with Zygmut is like passing kidney stones. But it's worth every ounce of pain. Fills my soul with a lot of pride."

Rusty laughed himself a little more out of tune, remembering the endless nights his owner spent cursing the name Zygmut. Claude routinely fired frustrated punches into the wall since he couldn't so much as write a second verse. Now Nashville's Shakespeare was under a deadline and hadn't slept in days.

Rusty noticed Claude's body went slack and loose. His grip eased like a dying man.

"J. Claude? Are you sleeping?"

"Hmmh?" his body sprung back to rigid life. "Hell, no, son. Keep yapping."

"Sure. Now, can you tell the readers about your inspiration for the project?"

"Well, my first big hit, back before I had about four-hundred gold records, was a song called Jeanine," Rusty could tell the singer was speaking with tight lips so the cigarette didn't drop. A black snow of ash fell over the guitar's body.

"Oh," the interviewer cleared his throat and sang in a flat voice.

Well I've tangoed in ballrooms
And sipped fine champagne
And I've slept in the ditches
I've huffed gasoline

There weren't nothing in my life
To fill that lonely ravine
Until I made you my wife
Lovely, sweet Jeanine

"Say, that's not half bad," Claude gave a friendly chuckle. "See, when I'd sing that song, girls in the crowd named Jeanine would always say how special it made them feel." Claude grabbed a fistful of his shirt's chest. "And I loved that. Little bottle rockets fired up my spine just seeing their smiles."

Rusty's tension eased to the point where his strings dropped terribly out of tune. This was the first honest thing his owner said and it reminded the guitar of days when it was just the two of them, building a cult following in hazy honky-tonks on Music Row just for the love of performing. Before that bus existed. Before Claude's hundred-dollar-a-day club sandwich habit came into the picture. Before a man in Clarksdale, Mississippi tried stealing everything from Nashville's Shakespeare.

"But I'd feel kind of crummy when the other pretty girls would ask, 'what about me?' and I didn't have a song for 'em. So I vowed on July Fourth, 1976, our nation's bicentennial, to make every girl on Earth smile."

Rusty's tuning pegs tightened the same way his owner's neck got stiff when he stressed. J. Claude's truthfulness hadn't lasted long and Rusty never expected it to. But the guitar burned up when his owner lied about why The Ladies' Project began. Nashville's Shakespeare never, ever, not once, mentioned that son-of-a-bitch thief in Clarksdale.

The reporter coughed, stubbed out his smoke and leaned forward: "Now, tell me about Rusty."

"Aw, come on. It's all been said many, many times."

"Please. Some readers might not know."

"What do you need to know, man? He's my best friend, my musical sidekick, and constant companion. Just like my voice, he soars like an angel and stings like Satan's pitchfork. I'd just as soon punch my mother in the mouth than let another person touch Rusty."

The guitar laughed, knowing those lines were actually true.

Martin Dobson's voice was uneasy, nearly groveling: "Pardon me, Claude. But why are there so many sandwiches on the floor?"

"My cleaning lady has hepatitis. Let's keep talking about ol' Rusty."

"Fair enough," the kid said, pointing his baffled face toward the floor. "Aren't guitars usually named for women?"

The purple ceiling tassels swung as the bus pulled into a truck stop. White parking lot lamps bullied past the velvet drapery. The men chewed on a long stretch of silence. Rusty was familiar with its bitterness.

"Most fellas, yeah. B.B. King's got Lucille. Willie Nelson's got Loretta. Kenny Rogers probably has some faggy-named guitar, I don't know. But Rusty here was actually owned by my departed wife. She named him a few years before dying in a motorcycle accident in 1977."

"Oh, I'm sorry. Gosh, I hope it wasn't a drunk driver."

"Nah, no way, not Stella." Rusty felt his owner's posture slump again. Claude clearly wanted to crawl into bed. "She was actually trying to jump seven busses at the Astrodome. I told her it was crazy. That skinny ass of hers could never build up the momentum…"

The bus left the gas pumps behind and J. Claude paused, seemingly lost in the curtain's wandering movement. Rusty sensed a familiar touch of heartbreak when his owner played a few tuneless notes. This time, the guitar tried extra hard to sound perfect for J. Claude.

"Let's switch gears." The reporter cleared his throat. "What can you tell me about Denny Dynasty?"

"Next question."

"What have you got to hide?"

"Not a damn thing."

"Then tell the readers about Denny Dynasty."

"Ha!" J. Claude laughed, but Rusty felt Caruthers' grip tighten, fingernails dug into the fretboard. "He's a hack, a copycat and a social deviant in my opinion. Probably even the Good Lord's opinion too."

The reporter's voice grew curious. "So you hate Dynasty because he's gay?"

"That's for God above to judge, not me," J. Claude said. Rusty sighed. The guitar knew Claude only referenced God to appeal to conservative fans. Judy was full of marketing advice like that. Caruthers didn't actually put much stock in a man's orientation and even took an online ministerial course to officiate the marriage of his stage manager, Barney Thackery, and his drummer, Paul Lutz. "Me, I personally can't stand the booger-nosed brat because he's stealing my idea."

"You don't think it's because in five short years, since he announced his songwriting project, Denny's written nearly as many loves songs about men as you have women?"

"Hell no," J. Claude said in a stiff, military roar. The bus must have found construction because its momentum entirely stopped dead.

"You don't think it's because he's been selling approximately twice as many albums as you? Or because people are calling him the next Hank Williams?"

"Har, the next Hank Williams," J. Claude's voice was dark and slippery. "Hank Williams with a manicure and a pink scarf, maybe."

Rusty thought about Denny Dynasty's well-trimmed fingers. The young singer briefly opened some shows for J. Claude a decade earlier, long before he came out of the rhinestone-studded closet and announced his songwriting odyssey. Rusty decided it wouldn't feel so bad to have a clean, skillful set of hands like Denny's run across his strings once in a while. It'd been nearly thirty-five years since another human was allowed to touch J. Claude's guitar. Arctic loneliness dominated Rusty's world. He may as well have been the last musical instrument on Earth. "Guitars," he thought, "aren't monogamous."

The bus growled its decades-old engine and built up speed. Orange construction flashers reflected on the purple walls.

"So, it's safe to say you two won't be sharing a cocktail after sharing the Country Music Awards stage tomorrow night?"

"I don't drink fuzzy navels, I only drink whiskey. Like a man. Next question."

The bus hit an enormous bump that launched both men a few inches above their seats. Club sandwich carcasses landed along the walls with soggy splats. Rusty spun from his owner's hand and klonked to a rest on the floor, leaning against the reporter's leg.

Touching another human filled Rusty with an emotion he abandoned years ago. Suddenly, a garden of beautiful flowers bloomed in his body. The guitar's heart knocked the dust off itself like it'd been in a coma the last three decades.

"Well, perhaps you'd like to read this statement Mister Dynasty released today," the kid passed a folded press release to Caruthers. "He says some interesting stuff."

"Oh, no thanks." Claude tried to return the letter.

"You aren't interested in Denny saying you are 'washed up,' your voice sounds 'like a blown tire' or that you look 'like Frankenstein without bolts'?"

Claude's face tightened and turned a nervous shade of wine. "Uh, no. I'm cool. Why don't you just read it? I can't find my glasses, plus you got one of those strong voices, like that dude who played Darth Vader."

"James Earl Jones…" The kid waggled the paper through the air, but J. Claude slid backward the way some do at the smell of rotten food. "Jay, I'm dying to know what you make of these accusations. Please, just have a look." The paper fell into Claude's lap again.

"Judy!" The singer screamed, a bullet of sweat dodged between forehead wrinkles. Then another. And so on.

"Mister Caruthers," the kid leaned forward and stuffed the recorder closer to Claude's face. "Is something wrong?"

"Interview over, hoss."

A redheaded burst of energy ran through the door and Rusty watched a familiar scene play out again. "Okay, thanks for riding along with us, Martin. J. Claude has to rest his vocal cords for tomorrow night, so he won't be answering any more—"

"Tell me I'm wrong—"

"You're wrong." Judy shook his hand and gently nudged the scribe from Claude's quarters.

"J. Claude doesn't own reading glasses does he?"

FOUR

"Science? Science is like pouring maple syrup on grits. You know what I'm saying?"
   -J. Claude Caruthers, *Nashville's Shakespeare*

"Yeah, launch me! Send me at a billion miles-an-hour, I dare you, you piece of shit." One proton was not happy about his new job. "Who do you think I am? Albert II?"

This microscopic shaving of energy was simply minding his own business—going to work, being a good husband to his proton wife and an excellent father to his proton children—when the particle was isolated for the Hadron Collider's initial run.

"Oh, you didn't think I knew about Albert II, did you? First monkey in space, maybe? You know why the original Albert wasn't in space? Cause that stupid chimp died on his way up. You know what happened to cute, fuzzy, little Albert II? He died too. Yeah, the US Army gave him a joyride on a V-2 rocket. So, just as he made the cover of *Great Achievements in Monkey History* magazine, he splattered back to the ground.

"And you know why?"

There was no answer from the proton's dark, frigid quarters.

"Because nobody asked him. Just like me, Alberts One and Two were plucked out of the millions of other options to be in some moronic experiment that had nothing to do with them.

"Do you think they let monkeys ride on spaceships now

28

that it's safe? Hell no. Do you think these knuckleheads at the Hadron Collider will thank me, little Mister Proton, once my face plows into another proton at the speed of oblivion?

"Shit, you know the answer."

This proton was loaded into his end of the collider without warning. The proton didn't have time to lock the front door or even give Mrs. Proton a kiss goodbye. Which would have been nice, because, as protons go, his wife, Audrey, was smoking hot. Not only that, but Mister Proton was going bowling with the guys that evening and being smashed into a bazillion subatomic particles certainly made winning the league championship tougher.

Things were cold and dark in the Collider. The temperature was far below freezing in order to mimic deep space. In order to mimic the beginning of the universe.

"'Doctor Caruthers,' I heard one of these lab-coated assholes say," the proton gave a whiny imitation human voice. "'I cannot believe our luck. I mean it's horrible what happened to the other team. Botulism. Wow, who would have guessed all of Team Orange would come down with severe food poisoning on the eve of their Hadron test?'"

"Then the other human, Caruthers, this bulldog-looking guy with a dumb ponytail was like, 'It's a shame, Karen.'" The proton made a deep voice like he'd heard surgeons on soap operas use. "'Then, get this, he goes: 'if I had to place a bet, I'd guess those doomsday creeps outside the lab poisoned Team Orange's food.'"

"'You're kidding.' this stupid broad said. 'I mean, they throw water balloons and chant and wave those signs about the end of the world, but food poisoning?'"

"'I'm as shocked as you. But these luddites and their apocalypse talk are capable of anything. I'm just glad we're down here, safe and sound.

"'Now, stay focused. I've isolated one proton, please check the second chamber.'"

The proton's dense anger kept him warm. "Doctor Caruthers, you are in for it now. I pray to the god of protons everywhere that your hand accidentally gets stuck in that seventeen mile track. You ever had one of my kind fired through your flesh faster than a bullet? It ain't good, friend. Oh, but it'll feel like busting a nut on my end." The proton started to laugh until he was coughing and his proton tummy got a cramp.

Outside his containment, Mister Proton heard strange noises—metallic clanking, electronic whirring, beeps and bloops from a dozen computers. This put a momentary end to revenge plans.

"Clear," he heard a scientist say.

"Check," another said.

"Begin countdown," that Doctor Caruthers asshole said.

By the time the proton realized he was traveling at the speed of light, the ride was nearly over. Humans couldn't even flick another's ear by the time a light speed proton traveled seventeen miles.

Mister Proton flew around the concrete track at a pace that would peel flesh from a body. The force compacted the proton until he was a dense pellet of energy. At the end of his journey, the proton was perfectly imitating the opening ceremonies of the universe, when a sight brought him to tears.

"Audrey?" he said, seeing his wife barreling toward him at the speed of light, lining up for one final goodbye kiss of Big Bang proportions.

FIVE

"Now, some of Nashville's prettiest ladies claim I have the strength of an entire Marine platoon, but I'm really only one guy. One handsome, handsome, strong-ass guy."
-J. Claude Caruthers, *Nashville's Shakespeare*

J. Claude opened stinging eyelids to the sound of a fist bullying the dressing room door. "What?" he screamed. "I was practically asleep." His energy was down to nothing. "Almost," he whined, staggering toward the lock and turning it.

The private backstage rooms at the Country Music Awards weren't much nicer than Claude's bedroom on the bus. Fewer half-eaten sandwiches lying around maybe, certainly a lot less purple velvet, but equal square footage. There was hardly space for anything beyond that evening's selection of cowboy hats and a comfortable leather couch. J. Claude covered his face when Judy flipped a switch and light stabbed his eyes.

"Sleeping?" her eyes grew big and excited as she entered the room. "Does that mean you're finished with Zygmut? Wow, pretty big day for the Caruthers men, if I say so," Judy swatted her boss' chest with a rolled newspaper.

A rush of chattering people passed Claude's open door. Backstage was traffic jammed with country music royalty, so many, in fact, that Caruthers—the evening's star performer—went unnoticed.

"No, I haven't written the song. I can't think of anything that rhymes with that stupid, horrible, dumb, ugly, fat chick's

31

name." He sat back on the soft leather sofa.

"Oh, well, maybe not such a big day." She leaned toward Caruthers and caught seriousness sparkling in his eyes. "Look, why not just write a song that doesn't rhyme?"

The man's face, a tributary of creases, dropped into his hands. "I can't."

"Sure you can."

"No, Judy. I can't. I don't know how to write songs that don't rhyme." His voice was a muffled whimper. This showcase of weakness startled Judy, it tensed her fingers. "I can't eat broccoli without wanting to puke. I hate people who are taller than me. And I can only sing in rhymes." He lifted his accusing face, "I ain't perfect, Judy. Happy?"

She was far from thrilled. Insomnia was clearly destroying the boss. She felt largely responsible.

Judy's tone was soft now. "Either way, you have to come up with something." She was ashamed of shattering this eggshell ego. "You're headlining the show. We've been promoting this as Zygmut's debut. People are expecting to hear your final song. Zygmut is all anybody can talk about. The crowd, jeez, the presenters and award winners have to shout to be heard. The audience is a pack of lunatics."

Those lunatics were five-thousand men in tuxedoes and women in sparkly, flowing gowns stacked from the floor to the rafters. The roar they created was actually an organized chant, screaming J. Claude's name over and over and over. A certain electricity tumbled from seat to seat, tickling the happiest places in the crowd's brain, causing even sore award losers to stand and holler and stomp boots.

This hurricane howl was a gentle murmur back in Claude's room.

"I just need a few winks." Claude fell back on the couch. He looked up at his publicist with a face of total pain. His skin was puffy and pale. His eyes consisted more of red veins than white space. Old sweat granules clung on his skin to the point where Judy breathed through her mouth. "I haven't been able to sleep, pushing that damn boulder up a hill, not to mention that little bastard Dynasty breathing down my..." he stopped and his body curled magnetically into a fetal fold. Hovering so close to sleep made his limbs tingle like sex.

"Boss, this is huge. Finishing the Ladies' Project on national television erases what happened in Missoula and probably covers you in advance for a few more screw ups."

"Just let me sleep. I'm not begging you, I'm telling you. Besides, I think I'm hallucinating." The little body wound tighter. "I thought you said today was good for the Caruthers men." His eyes perked, they always did when the subject was J. Claude Caruthers' greatness. He quoted his autobiography: "'Now, some of Hollywood's prettiest ladies claim I have the strength of an entire Marine platoon, but I'm really only one guy.' There are no Caruthers men."

"I did say men, look at the paper." A smug grin crossed the publicist's face. "Lloyd did it. For a day, your brother is just as famous as you. Maybe even more so."

Claude flipped open the paper as Judy shut the door with a stern crack.

"The headline says: 'Physicist Recreates Big Bang.'"

"Yippee." Caruthers nearly asked if Judy ever got that special twenty-four hour gun license, because this didn't qualify as Claude-waking material in his book. His trigger finger throbbed itchy.

"A manmade Big Bang is a huge deal, Claude. The President wants to meet Lloyd."

The warped skin around J. Claude's throat tightened. Disgusted gurgles worked out his mouth.

Judy assumed heartburn was haunting the boss. She went to the medicine cabinet for antacid when he spoke: "This President never offered to meet me. Met all the others presidents, but not this S-O-B. I swear, Capitol Hill has the worst taste in music." His hand scratched through the couch cushions for a pack of cigarettes. "Remember that Clinton guy?"

"President…Bill Clinton?" her brow dipped and she put away the Tums. "Yeah, I remember."

"Had Fleetwood Mac play his inauguration. Shit, talk about tone deaf. I'd rather see that momma's boy Kenny Rogers—"

"Stop it. We're talking about Lloyd. We should send him congratulations. A letter, an email, something nice. He sounds like an amazing man. Here's a great opportunity to reconnect."

"What part of 'estranged from my family' don't you understand? I swear, Judy, some days your neck must ache like hell, because that head is nothing but concrete." He found, lit and puffed on a cigarette. The tangy smell eased those nerves a shade.

Judy marveled at how quickly the room thickened with smog. "Look, I'm just here to make sure you get that song written. You need something, anything." She waved a petite hand in front of her face. "You take the stage in two hours, so worse comes to worst, just ad-lib something. You don't have much time. Plus, another group of Caruthers' Kids are coming by, so let's clean this dump up." She began another club sandwich roundup, shoveling bread and meat into her arms. "Put that cigarette out. Think about their little lungs."

J. Claude's imagination danced with shiny silver revolvers wiping Judy's smile away. Wiping away her fascination with that stupid asshole Lloyd. Damn that judge for taking away his Second Amendment rights just when he needed them most. Last J. Claude heard, his entire firearms collection was sold at some police auction. Apparently one bidder snatched up the whole lot. He still had tons of obsessed fans like that. Claude-Hoppers, they were called.

Judy bent down to pick up another club sandwich and Claude saw the scar on the back of her arm. The spaghetti straps of Judy's black cocktail dress revealed a thin pink gash and dots where the stitches held. Those brief gun fantasies disappeared because aches about that bullet still fermented in his tank. Caruthers thought this was a good time to finally apologize. He cleared his throat and ran through a mental script. When his lips split to speak, only a bubble of hot air passed. Nashville's Shakespeare holstered that imaginary revolver and decided to be nice instead.

"Let me grab that," he stole the plate. "Go get me a coffee and I'll sign autographs until the end of time. I promise. It'll be good for my image, right? And, you know, grab something expensive for yourself at the bar. Get an extra one of those fancy-pants gift bags."

"Thanks," her voice was dull and bored as she opened the door. "You do realize drinks are free backstage, right?"

"I know you really like that bubbly wine stuff."

"It's called champagne, Claude. And, yes, I do like it. I love it. And I'm going to grab an entire bottle from room service once this night is over." She slammed the door with another tight crack.

Just as swiftly, the door notched open and her voice shot through: "Lyrics, write those lyrics. Chop chop." The door went closed again.

Caruthers found Rusty and focused, letting that violent urge to sleep disappear. Claude didn't have any children, but holding that guitar in his arms felt just as warm and rewarding as a baby boy. Nashville's Shakespeare tried to write the song, but his mind was gritty and littered like the highway shoulders he crisscrossed each night. His eyes couldn't focus, words swirled and flushed through his mind and his fingers plucked chords that hadn't been invented yet.

This was every day of his life since finishing that second-to-last song, one about girls named Zelma. Writer's block made J. Claude's hands shake with anxiety. It kept him from sleeping. He barely ate. Caruthers once told Rusty, when the entire bus had gone to bed, that the last few years were like he had to sneeze but couldn't. There was a strange buildup inside and he could imagine the release of finishing, but nothing came except frustration.

He twanged a klutzy note on the guitar and sighed a familiar mantra. Leaning back, slipping a hat over his eyes, J. Claude Caruthers used his favorite autobiography quote, the words that helped him survive this paralyzing bout of blockage.

"Why try when you can quit, old boy?"

Lately, it was his default answer. Quitting was easier than stressing. Eventually, he assumed, the song would come. He was simply pushing it too hard. A nap was the perfect prescription.

J. Claude told his eyes to quit. He told his ears to quit. He ordered his mind to quit. He demanded his aching muscles throw in the towel, as well. Caruthers massaged arthritic knuckles and tried to forget all the fans eagerly awaiting that song. The more he forgot all the potentially happy people, the more restless he became.

A secret relief overwhelmed Claude with a knock on his door. When simply quitting wasn't enough, distractions from Zygmut were worth their weight in gold.

A troupe of boys and girls marched into his dressing room, wearing identical blue Caruthers' Kids shirts. The class of ten-year-olds stood nearly as tall as the country star.

"Howdy, there. Don't be shy, come on in." Claude rubbed his eyes and shined up his voice, trying to draw smiles from the stunned crowd. He was used to this reaction, especially with children.

Claude Crunch was in every cereal aisle, J. Claude's Justice Rangers had been a Saturday morning cartoon staple for years and his voice was the centerpiece of that album about famous fairy tale chicks. These kids probably thought Claude was about as real as Daffy Duck.

"I hear you little ones are going to watch me play some songs tonight. Well, gosh, I sure appreciate it."

The kids were all plucked from inner city orphanages and

sent to a special educational development center. J. Claude sponsored the entire operation, from the schoolhouse, to the teachers' salaries, to the children's uniforms. Nashville's Shakespeare loved it so much he didn't even try to write it off on taxes. For years, Caruthers felt helpless watching kids with childhoods just as empty and unhappy as his own. His money had been tied up with that son-of-a-bitch in Clarksdale over the last few decades; J. Claude was only recently able to afford assistance for those less fortunate. Caruthers' Kids seemed like the perfect way to help. Since its inception, over 300 youngsters graduated the program.

"But you know," he said with a soft voice fit for reading Jack and the Beanstalk. "I need to warm up my hand for guitar picking. You all think you can help me?"

The kids were fidgety but seemed curious. One brave girl with black braids spoke up, "How, Mister J. Claude?"

"Glad you asked, miss," now the country legend's voice was as bright as his smile. "Signing autographs really helps. You all wouldn't happen to have some pictures for me to sign, would you? That'd sure make my day."

The children screamed and waved eight-by-ten glossy headshots of Claude. His celebrity transferred that wild awards show electricity via these little ones. It made Claude grin. It didn't hurt that the photos were good, too, taken back when he still had bushy hair and routinely got a decent night's rest.

For nearly an hour, he talked with each child individually, told them how special they were and inked encouraging notes.

Just as the kids began impatiently crawling around the dressing room, the air disappeared from J. Claude's lungs. A man poked his head in and Caruthers nearly tossed a little girl at him.

"Hiya handsome," said a peppy voice that could have belonged to a cruise ship activities director. "You're looking lovely tonight. And me, well, you don't have to say anything. I think we both know." The man curtseyed as if wearing a gown.

"Dynasty!" Claude shouted, which quickly made his throat ragged. "Get out of here." Caruthers stood and the child on his lap fell to the floor with a joyful squeal. He studied Denny Dynasty from shiny boots to pink scarf to greased haircut and made a curious face: "Wait, first, what the hell is the bright idea with that costume?"

Denny Dynasty, thin, trim and wearing way too much eye-liner, did a catwalk spin for the crowd. His skin-tight white jumpsuit showcased a strip of purple sequins running up the legs and down the arms. A wider band of sparkly purple splashed across the chest. The shade perfectly matched J. Claude's bedroom décor.

"This old thing," he blushed, or maybe he just applied too much rouge. "Just something I wear when I want to feel strong and brave. Just like my hero."

"You bastard."

"I knew you'd recognize this getup."

A murmuring group built outside the open dressing room door, heads in the back bobbed for a better view. The frightened children at J. Claude and Denny's feet plastered themselves against the wall as if the two men were made of Brussels sprouts and booster shots.

"If you continue to spit on my wife's grave, so help me," J. Claude paused, realizing a child was tugging his shirt.

"Mister J. Claude, sir," the girl with braids said in an innocent voice. "You're hurting my hand."

Claude realized he'd been shaking her hand before Denny arrived. He released the paw and apologized.

The white and purple outfit was identical to one Stella wore. "Spit on her grave? Sugar, this is a tribute to the finest stuntwoman the world ever saw. Stella Caruthers was my hero growing up. It's just a funny coincidence you and I and a special guest have to share the stage singing one of your ridiculous songs. Which, by the way, I dropped by to get the sheet music for. What asinine tune are we singing tonight? Beatrice, Linda,

Darlene? Not that Rapunzel one from your," he looked suspiciously at the Caruthers' Kids, "children's album."

J. Claude stepped close enough to smell Denny's peppermint lip gloss. The crowd at the door ooooooohed. "Maybe I'll sing one about this lady I beat to death once. It's called Denny, You dumb piece of—"

"Hey, hey," Judy wiggled through the crowd tossing elbows, but managing to keep J. Claude's coffee upright. The pressure in the room released. "Knock it off you two. Break it up." She wedged between both singers. "Denny, I'll give some sheet music to your assistant. You'd better go and warm up your voice."

Denny stepped back and glared. "Don't need to, I'll sound like Waterford Crystal looks when I trade verses with J. Corpse Caruthers." Dynasty's manicured finger pointed to the rumpled, tired singer.

"That don't even make sense." J. Claude looked at his boots, shaking his head.

"Awwwwww," the disappointed crowd broke up.

"Your sister told me you wouldn't get that comment," Dynasty said with an inside-joke chuckle.

J. Claude's eyes burned with anger and insomnia, "I don't have a sister."

"That's funny, because I've been spending a lot of time with a woman a few years older than you. Goes by the name Zygmut Caruthers. Familiar?"

J. Claude's chest hadn't felt a shock like that since taking a bullet for Jimmy Carter at Farm Aid '89. A little known fact that Caruthers omitted from his autobiography was that Claude actually tried pushing Kenny Rogers into the line of fire, but failed. Caruthers cut it from Nashville's Shakespeare because it contradicted the book's message of, "if you put your mind to stuff, you can probably do it." Plus, the illustrations looked like crap.

"Man, all that makeup sure makes you look old," Claude

grinned, secretly praying to change the subject. "Or maybe fat. I sure as hell can't tell which one's worse."

The purple and white suit made a lightning quick lunge toward Caruthers before stopping abruptly. "Denny!" Judy yelled, nudging the singer. "Scram." She fixed a stray dangle of red hair that fell loose during the struggle.

"I'm not leaving until your friend here apologizes," Denny said in a fantastic diva voice. The same voice he perfected in the lead role of Auntie Mame on Broadway.

Before Judy's lips formed a word, J. Claude casually stuck a finger in her face. "I can handle this." The singer lowered to a knee and motioned for the children to circle him. "Which one of you buckaroos wants to earn fifty dollars?"

The kids leaped up and down, screaming.

"Shhhhh, shhhh, shhh, shhhh," Claude hushed the nervy pack. "Now everyone look careful at Mister Dynasty here," the group focused attention toward the man in purple and white. Dynasty gave an unamused, but slightly nervous, smirk. "See how nice his face looks? See how beautiful his eyes are?"

"He's prettier than my last foster momma," one orphan said.

"Well, I have a crisp fifty waiting for the first one of you special, smart, wonderful boys and girls who brings back Denny Dynasty's pretty fake eyelashes."

A moment of tense silence hung as everyone involved considered the offer.

Denny studied these children and made a yip like one of those dogs J. Claude saw women carrying in purses. The white and purple singer sprinted from the room with a rumbling, giggling pack of children close behind.

"Y'all put your mind to stuff," Claude yelled to the gang of kiddies. "You can probably do it."

J. Claude flopped back onto his couch with a huge smile that momentarily erased insomnia and stress. The thought of his enemy being beaten by grade schoolers wrapped a warm blanket of happiness over the singer. Those emotions had been mostly cold since Stella died. It was a lively sensation that used to visit him nightly when his boots clacked across a stage and stepped before a microphone.

That would be about the only part of this life he'd miss once he finished writing Zygmut's song. He'd been promising himself for years that the day he put the Ladies' Project to bed, he could finally hang himself from a closet with an extension cord. Thoughts of death delivered a strange calm whenever he desperately needed one.

Judy playfully slapped him on the back and spread that comfortable blanket even further around the sleepy singer. "I suppose those kids do need some positive encouragement."

"That's what I'm here for," he chuckled as thoughts of self-inflicted death disappeared.

Claude made a quick scan around the empty dressing quarters, and that blanket of happiness caught fire and burned his skin. His stomach coiled with anxious pain. The room was too empty.

"Rusty." His throat was a raw, panicked bark. "Where the hell is Rusty?"

SIX

"Someone once said, 'You got to have smelt a lot of mule manure before you can sing like a hillbilly.' I'm pretty sure that was me. Must've been crazy drunk when I said it."
 -J. Claude Caruthers, *Nashville's Shakespeare*[2]

When the frustration set in, the waxy smell of blown birthday candles was everywhere. The music had a festive bounce. The paper streamers hung in bright colors, but Lloyd's spirit was charred black.

He was used to it, though.

Every pat on the shoulder and comment about the first collision's spectacular success was a crushing reminder of failure. The physicist badly wanted a distraction. For the thousandth time in his celebrated scientific career, Lloyd was climbing a steep and slippery mountain. He'd never reach the top, plant a flag and say: "Yes, I've accomplished something." This was the rusted faucet his life's disappointment leaked from. Solving one scientific riddle always birthed countless more difficult ones. "Whenever science closes a door," he preached to naïve lab assistants. "Life kicks in about a hundred windows."

What was that smug bastard Oppenheimer thinking when the first atom bomb whitewashed the desert in light? That was a success, a clear-cut move forward. Lloyd assumed that marvelous feeling was the same one J. Claude felt every time he

---

2 Upon further research, the author discovered this was actually first said by Hank Williams Sr.

recorded another hit record. These dense, painful ideas gave the bronze champagne in Lloyd's hand a spoiled milk flavor.

Lloyd's Green Team was celebrating deep underground, in the Collider's largest meeting room. Snacks and booze and music filled every crevice of the space. The board of directors even arrived with the mayor of the nearest Swiss village. They presented Lloyd with a key to the city. Doctor Caruthers' eyes were specks from constant photo snaps. He felt rotten for smiling and pretending to be proud.

Pausing for another photo and shaking some stranger's hand, a quote crept into his mind: "I have become death, the shatterer of worlds."

Lloyd had forgotten almost everything he'd learned from reading an Oppenheimer biography decades earlier. But now he remembered this line—a scrap of Hindu scripture the bomb's father uttered upon seeing a man-made sun burst across Los Alamos.

Caruthers shook more hands and said hello to women by kissing their cheeks. All the while, a disappointment hardened—his scientific leap wasn't as dramatic as Oppenheimer's. So bland it didn't deserve a powerful phrase. "Even if something amazing did happen," he teased, "I'm not clever enough to quote scripture. Stupid J. Claude could probably whip something up, though."

Caruthers craved a distraction because nothing really happened that day. Nothing ever seemed to happen in physics. When the two protons collided, there was a microscopic burst so fast and dull his scientists needed their billion dollar computers to even notice. That bang didn't unwrap a gift containing the mysteries of the universe. Rather, Team Green quickly determined it would take thousands of little explosions and years of research to draw even the most basic conclusion about Earth's origins. It left Caruthers deflated. The parameters and rules of science were some kind of glass bubble squeezing tighter and tighter as he grew older. And for what? He had no wife, no children. Lloyd told himself in weak moments that science would care for him, he didn't need a family.

Veronique walked past the open door with her window squeegee, providing a diversion from the handshakes and noisemakers and thin plastic Collision Course for Success! banners. "Need a hand?" Lloyd said, out in the peaceful hallway. He rolled up lab coat sleeves and watched the woman's deep brown eyes widen, startled.

"I think a hand is all you can lend," her face went shocked and embarrassed.

The joke didn't bother Lloyd. He cleared his throat, growing tender.

"Sorry, I didn't mean…I think you need to go celebrate," she smiled and her round cheeks pushed from her face. "You are the most famous man on the planet right now. You are slightly overqualified to wash windows." The squeaking sponge soaped a pane of glass.

Lloyd took a large breath and watched her eyes blink with a mysterious enthusiasm.

Caruthers made a nervous cough and pretended to admire the large clean window overlooking a portion of collider track—nothing, a tangle of wires and piping. "I think I'd rather spend time here…" he gulped, squeezing colon muscles. Lloyd's experience with women was pitifully minimal. He had only asked out three girls before. Two turned him down and the other eventually requested a restraining order. "With you."

Veronique's head lifted. The light met her hair and face: She looked like a sculpture in church. Lloyd's body was suddenly traveling supersonic around a seventeen-mile loop. His bowels pinched tighter, waiting for the inevitable collision—the inevitable rejection.

Lloyd was close enough to enjoy a final whiff of her lemon cleaner aroma.

Surprisingly, the janitor passed the squeegee, her straight white teeth showing some carefree glee that was a mystery to

Lloyd. "Only if you explain how this thing works," Veronique pointed to the window showcasing seventeen miles of Lloyd's disappointment.

"Fair enough." For the first time, in the physicist's eyes, the collider's grey concrete lines of failure and multi-colored wires of missed expectations looked like fun. "But only if you tell me about yourself."

"Let's start the tour," Veronique said.

He grinned and cocked his head, waiting for the punch line. "Around the entire circuit?"

"Yes, of course."

"I have to make that walk about once a week. It takes almost six hours, trust me."

Veronique thought it over and locked her gentle arm within Lloyd's. "That's alright, I'll walk it with you."

Caruthers battled his knees as they attempted a collapse. The astrophysicist's heart got its act together and continued a hefty beat. "Well, let's start where everything ends and see how much energy you have for the entire loop."

"Where the bang happened?"

"I wouldn't call it that. More like a burp. But, yeah, basically."

The pair took lazy steps toward the lab where two protons met and created the world's most underwhelming Big Bang. He did most of the talking. Not about physics, though. Veronique was incredibly curious about the scientist, as if she'd been waiting to pepper Lloyd with questions, but never had the nerve.

"My family? Mmmmmpphhhhhhhh…" An uncomfortable chuckle bounced around the empty hall. Thick fingers buttoned and unbuttoned a shirt cuff. "We're a little scattered. My brother, he's…" Lloyd stopped and tilted his head, "we haven't spoken in years. You've probably heard of J. Claude Caruthers, the singer."

"Who?" Her accent was tiny and streamlined. Her honest face was stunning.

Lloyd's entire life had been trapped beneath the cold, dark shadow of his brother. Since J. Claude slid from the womb four minutes after Lloyd, this beautiful Swiss janitor was the first person who didn't seem to know the infamous Caruthers twin.

A lightheaded, woozy grin dominated his face. "It doesn't matter. My brother's very busy. I have a sister too, a few years older. But she took off with my parents when Claude and I were in high school."

"Your parents abandoned you?" she gave his arm a sympathetic rub that burned through skin with a tingle. Veronique's delicate fingers lingered a moment when they met Lloyd's rubber hand.

"Probably," he said, rolling his eyes. "Nobody's really sure if they abandoned us. The police never tracked them down. One day our parents and sister just vanished. I think they were members of a church, like, hardcore members of this…I always assumed it was a church. Claude and I never knew how to classify the thing. We just sort of…"

In front of the lab door, before Lloyd could input his security code, the tall janitor stepped in close and bent to his level. Her lips were warm on Lloyd's cold, stunned set. Her hair fell into his face and smelled like clean laundry. The kiss wasn't long, but some atom bomb deep within Lloyd exploded into a twirling universe of red hot emotion. For the first time, the rules and parameters of science weren't so claustrophobic. He saw his future in that instant. He wanted the wife and the kids. He wanted to be remembered for more than a soul-butchering work ethic.

"Poor, poor baby," she ran a soft finger across Lloyd's burning cheek. "No family, no hand. But look at what you've accomplished." She nuzzled his neck. "I'm very proud of you." Her lips grazed his ear, the hair on his neck spiked.

Lloyd trembled until his rubber hand nearly wiggled off. His throat cleared, "—and here is where the two protons collided," he tapped in a code and opened the door, praying the boredom of science would cool his nerves. "Ta-da."

The doorknob stung when Lloyd turned it. This jolt of pain was quickly surrounded by cold. Not just cold, but frigid. He gave a moment's hesitation. However, the world's most famous astrophysicist had larger concerns. It was nuzzling that ear again.

The moment love sunk an arrow into Lloyd's chest wasn't like books and movies made it sound. There was no urge to strip Veronique naked across the cold white tile. Actually, the physicist nearly threw up with the urge to run. But a series of hazy images, like marriage and kids, kept his feet planted.

When they walked through the door his body turned more frigid than Veronique's massaging hand on his back. The pair watched a tan leather desk chair roll across the empty room. Lloyd's body tensed each time its wheels made tiny mouse squeaks. Shivers razored up Lloyd's back as paperclips and pencils zipped by rows of computer monitors. Loose sheets of paper flapped through the air the way perfect white seagulls dive-bomb for fish.

"Lloyd, do you believe in ghosts?" the janitor said, blindly scratching down his arm until finding that hand.

The glass bubble of Lloyd's world began squeezing again, staring at what used to be the main control monitor. The white plastic computer screen and its surrounding array of multicolored buttons and switches seemed to be disappearing.

"This isn't a ghost," Lloyd replied, knowing precisely what was happening. His eyes squinted so hard he didn't even notice the dream woman crushing his fake hand like a dog's jaw around a chew toy.

The lab walls were frosted, the desks sparkled with an icy sheen and a dance of fog exited his lips.

"Is this what I think it is?" Veronique took a brave step across mother of pearl tiles. She marveled as the rolling chair met the dark smudge along the wall. The chair, like the papers and pens ripping across the room, briefly transformed into a red glow before disappearing entirely.

"It can't be." Lloyd felt a familiar sting where his hand used to be. Phantom pains, the doctor called them, came when he was stressed. The missing hand sizzled like a thousand exposed nerves along his invisible palm and knuckles and fingers. "It's not scientifically possible. I ruled it out."

The black hole seemed lazy and kind of bored. Matter orbited around it, flashing crimson and fading into darkness. The room was anchored by a weird magnetic pull.

Lloyd and Veronique took a step closer as pens and rubber bands made bullet shots through crystallizing air. The entire room ached with cold. On the wall, a dry erase board's screws popped and it flapped with the rapid force of a sparrow's wing.

Lloyd felt the pull heavier on his body. If he closed his eyes, the scientist might have guessed a rope was tied around his waist with someone tugging.

"We must go, we need to run," he said in a strong voice.

"Yes," Veronique's lips shook. "We need to tell." Her words were sucked into anti-matter. "The police?"

"Don't worry." The gravitational yank popped off his rubber hand as he stepped backward.

"Oh, Lloyd," Veronique looked embarrassed for him, as if it was somehow her fault. "I'm sorry."

"Let's go now." He cycled his good hand through the air.

Veronique made a movement toward the prosthetic hand when the heavy dry erase board snapped from its wall and kicked violently into her spine.

She spun and fell across the tile with a dark "ooooff," as the board tumbled into the hole, flashing, blood-colored. Bits of paper and more clips singed a line through the laboratory, straight toward the exact point the two protons collided.

Lloyd stood helpless the moment her long blonde hair lifted straight up and pointed to that spot. "Lloyd?" A red glow reflected off of Veronique's wet face as a flood of tears formed. Her pale hand grasped empty air, reaching toward the physicist. The other hand's fingernails chipped in half, digging into the tile.

His body froze. His mind held idling.

Veronique slowly picked herself off the ground and stood with knees wobbly. Cracked fingernails bled at the tips.

Lloyd's knees were cement.

She held the rubber hand toward Lloyd. Veronique's arms shook.

That fleshy stump stayed at his side. A cloud of glacial breath hung before Lloyd's face. Those warm thoughts of transcending physics and starting a family were nowhere to be found now. The scientist's mind was a dark, empty void.

Veronique's balance tipped in the opposite direction. Her eyes, filled with shock and veins, grew plump.

Lloyd's balance, though his mind was starting to thaw with rescue thoughts, held with statue firmness.

It all ended before Lloyd could properly wrap his mind around it. One second Veronique was there, calling his name, taking a step. The next second, nothing remained but a red flicker and lemon cleaner smell. The rubber hand, limp on the white floor.

Another scrap from Oppenheimer's biography flashed red in his mind and then faded black. Reflecting upon the danger he and the Manhattan Project created, J. Robert Oppenheimer said, "the physicists have known sin and this is a knowledge which they cannot lose."

SEVEN

"Yeah, I'd say I'm just about the biggest partier in history. Maybe me, Caligula and that dude who invented moonshine."

-J. Claude Caruthers, *Nashville's Shakespeare*

"I've only seen J. Claude this upset two or three other times in my entire life," the tour bus thought. Its long body gently shook down the highway. In night's blackness, Nashville grew less populated, more rural. Out in no-man's land, midnight darkened trees gradually replaced the orange hum of street lamps. The smell of moist leaves was musky and deep.

The musical legend was stretched face-down on his velvet bedspread, sobbing so hard his golden throat grew dark. He pounded a fist into the mattress and a chorus of spring-loaded chirps melded with his crying.

"Claude," the bus heard Judy say, patting her boss' back. "Calm down, it wasn't that bad."

"That bad?" he lifted a blushing, mucky face. "That little purple bastard ripped me to shreds. I never had a crowd look at me like that."

"Like what?" His spasming shoulder muscles were flu-hot to touch.

"With all that…" the next word was stretched and grotesque, a pull of bloody taffy: "disappointment." J. Claude rubbed moisture from his eyes and slugged back whatever leaked from his nose. "God, it hurt. All the audience wanted was one stupid song and I blew it. On top of everything, Dynasty stole the show." His shoulders hiccupped and the wrinkled webbing under his eyes filled with tears. "I'm dead, Judy. We might as well sell the bus for scrap, I'm finished."

The bus' exhaust gave a nervous cough. It knew J. Claude would never sell, but still, even when you're built from several tons of steel, words hurt.

Just like when Caruthers considered getting a newer model a few years back, the bus took comfort knowing the singer's bank account was a ghost town. Driving Nashville's Shakespeare from gig to gig was the only life it ever knew. For god's sake, the name, "Nashville's Shakespeare" was airbrushed onto its sidepanels. That'd be like removing a tattoo.

"Let me get you a glass of scotch, something to calm you down," Judy said.

"Booze?" the singer's lips were a confused curl.

"I think there's some vodka, if that'd be better."

"You know I gave that shit up for Jesus."

Judy grinned, waiting for the joke. But Caruthers' expression didn't change. "When was the last time you went to church?" she stood with hands on hips. Copper hair, a tangle of vines tripping over her shoulders. Impatient tongue running across lips.

"Church? No, man." He took a deep breath and snorted back the tears. "Jesus Dominguez, best chef I ever had. The dude's on the bus all day. Don't pretend you don't know him. Man, that's racist."

"You gave up drinking for your chef?" Curiosity slowly pulled her closer. "That's news."

"You know me, I used to be up all hours of the night, boozing, drugging, screwing, partying. Jesus threatened to leave if I asked him to make another club sandwich at three in the morning. What's a man to do?"

"You're joking."

"Quit my evil ways that day. C'mon, don't you pay any attention around here?"

"A sandwich. You quit drinking for a sandwich?" Skepticism shook her face. The bus sped around a curve and she anchored her body against the night stand. "I wasn't concerned about your drinking. You've honestly never been all that crazy, Claude."

"Didn't you ever read my book? There's a whole damn chapter about it."

"Oh," her voice was dense. "Sure, of course. Right. I loved it."

"I bet." The talk seemed to calm the singer, especially where tears were concerned. He sat, slouch-shouldered, on his bed, looking at the purple ceiling. "I'm a wild man," he said with a convictionless huff.

"Fine, you're wild." She moved to the window, wanting to avoid this.

"Like a black bear." His nose snuffed, his eyes begged for reassurance.

"Sure, okay."

"But it's more than just food for this bear." Judy watched the soft man harden back to his normal self. "That dude is my best friend. Hell, my only friend. Ever since Jesus sat me down one night and said, 'Claude, quit trying to kill yourself.'" The singer's face was smooth, like remembering a dream. "He said, 'You're gonna live forever, so relax.'"

"Listen, Black Bear. You've never been out of control. Frankly, you're boring." Slowly, she moved across the cramped room to the tall chair, crossed her legs and looked down on Claude with curiosity. "In fact, I don't know if I've ever seen you have a conversation with the chef. This doesn't make sense."

"That's what I said. I don't understand. I was about two seconds away from telling Jesus to shut the hell up and not to forget the fancy mustard. But I chewed on it and realized that dude was talking about living forever through my music, through my legacy." He removed a studded cowboy hat and the light locked his eyes with sincerity. A naked spot of flesh crowned his head. "My fans know I held life by the shirt collar and punched its lights out. If I was going to tell my tale, I couldn't keep popping pills, chugging whiskey and bustin' dudes out of prison. That's a one-way ticket to the tomb."

"Seriously, I'm here all day, every day. That doesn't sound like you. You want people to imagine you're a wild man or a black bear, but it's not—"

"Jesus helped me realize I already have a legacy. And a pretty damn good one. So I turned my life down to a manageable volume. I like the idea of people remembering me as that fresh-faced kid with the long hair and the mustache, singing about all the women of the world when everybody knew he just lost his one true love. I don't want to choke on my own drunk vomit or die of AIDS from all my freaky sex. That ain't no decent way to be remembered. Folks still think I'm some hard-charging, heartbroken fool. Why change that? It's nice."

Judy's mouth dropped a little, unsure how to respond.

J. Claude dug a smoldering cigarette from the ashtray and kicked back across the bed. "So I'm set to live forever. I got a reputation as big as my gold record collection. I just can't do anything to put a ding on my legacy. Looking like a fool next to Denny Dynasty is a pretty big dent. Not finishing Zygmut is another. I can live with Dynasty, but if I don't finish the Ladies' Project, I got no control over how folks remember me. If folks remember me."

The sight of this broken hero made the bus lonely, like it was the only vehicle on an endless stretch of unlit highway. It hated the thought of becoming spare parts and not leaving its own mark on the history books.

This depressing scene reminded the cruiser of J. Claude's first breakdown. That moment was burned into the purple bus' memory.

J. Claude's record company purchased the bus for the singer in 1977. It was a well-known industry fact that Caruthers had no money, so transportation needed to be taken care of. Stella Caruthers painted the bus in sparkly purple from bumper to bumper that summer. She loved purple, it was her favorite. The husband and wife were doing a package tour where Stella performed stunts and then J. Claude would play a concert. The climax of each night was Stella jumping her motorcycle over Claude during his encore.

The tour was successful from May through August. Stadiums sold out, the stunt and music crews got along great and audiences left with smiles on their faces. Mr. and Mrs. Caruthers got along well too: they were trying to have a little Caruthers. The bus hated being nosy, but it was impossible to miss their nightly lovemaking right there in the back, atop the violet bedding.

The first time Stella and Claude failed to make love that summer was the night an ambulance carried the stuntwoman away. "Oh, Claude," the young bus thought during that evening. "I am so sorry." The singer lay on that same purple velvet blanket, sobbing for his lost wife.

"Hey," Judy told the present-day sobbing man, moving like she wasn't sure whether to wrap arms around Claude. "Don't worry. We'll find Rusty. And we'll fix your legacy. I live for this kind of damage control." She leaned down and gave Claude a gentle kiss where that famous long hair used to reside. Hair a stuffy Italian wigmaker once offered fifteen-thousand dollars for, according to the multiple chapters dedicated to J. Claude's coiffeur in *Nashville's Shakespeare.* "Look on the bright side," her voice was full of optimism. "People are not going to remember anything about Missoula once video of the Country Music Awards passes around the internet."

One other time the bus saw its owner cry was when a homely, squat female reporter from the *New York Times* asked why Lloyd wasn't mentioned in J. Claude's autobiography. "'Cause he didn't make me the man I am today. I made me the man I am today. Me and Stella."

It was the 1980s and J. Claude was country's biggest star. He looked remarkably similar to his current incarnation, only the bald spot was less severe. "So, your twin brother losing a hand because of your negligence had no effect on Nashville's Shakespeare?" she said.

"None," J. Claude flicked a cigarette butt into the purple carpet.

"I don't know, that sounds pretty Shakespearian." The reporter silently watched the singer.

"Where do you get this stuff?" J. Claude squinted and hopped off his tall chair. His nose was a breath from the reporter's. "Let's just talk about my book. Have you checked out the chapters on my hair? Pretty sweet illustrations, huh?"

"I get this stuff from research. And I'd rather talk about what's not in your book. Like, say," she let this hang in the air for a moment. "Why you and Lloyd were doing some science experiment a week after your mother, father and sister disappeared?"

Nashville's Shakespeare was instantly transformed into a sobbing blob with tears spilling down his face. He hadn't thought about that moment in decades. "His hand," Claude hollered like that time he pulled one of Jesus' casseroles out of the oven without mitts. "It was my fault."

Judy stood and slightly regretted giving her boss that kiss, though it did seem to comfort him. "How about I get Jesus to make you a club, hmmmm? You think a bite would make you feel better?"

"Yeah, okay," he said. Claude shooed her off, snuffling and running a sleeve across his nose.

A minute of silence and motionless thought helped calm the singer's nerves. He stopped shaking and coughing goo. The bus sensed nightmares of that Awards ceremony die down and were replaced with the urge to sleep.

Caruthers flipped off the lights and slipped under lilac sheets.

Just as his eyes were shut and that wave of darkness and rejuvenating sleep was near, the phone rang. Caruthers shot up with a nasty face. "I'll get it," his publicist said from the front of the bus.

"Nah, don't worry," J. Claude felt guilty once again and wanted to make Judy's life a little easier. He cleared throat phlegm and lifted a proud chin. "Hello?"

The phone silently buzzed for a few bumps on the road. J. Claude smiled and sniffled his nose at a comforting scent: Jesus crisping wheat toast.

"J. Claude Caruthers?" a raspy woman's voice said.

"I got no comment on tonight's performance," he leaned against his pillow and rubbed his raw nose again. "My publicist is handling all calls regarding—"

"I am not a reporter," the woman said, sounding offended. "Don't you recognize my voice?"

"Of course, sweetheart," J. Claude applied a vocal form-letter he saved for unfamiliar women. "How've you been? Are you still, you know, living in…" he took a stab, "Tucson?"

She filled the phone with a disgusted huff. "If you want to see that stupid guitar of yours again, you better remember this voice in the next thirty seconds."

The bus sensed its owner cringe and dig frightened fingers into the mattress. The Airstream considered accidentally shutting off its phone lines. But just like Claude, it was too shocked to react and simply listened to the raspy woman's story.

EIGHT

"You put your mind to stuff, you can probably do it."
  -J. Claude Caruthers, *Nashville's Shakespeare*

"Owee, owee, owee, my fingers," Lloyd's prosthetic hand said.

The black hole had grown a touch, getting fat and happy from swallowing its surroundings. The hand was next on the menu.

The hand was scared and upset after surviving such a lifetime of torment: Lloyd's rebellious years of "nubbing" it were tough, the prosthesis scare of 1998 with the "Robo-Mandible 2K" was tougher and, most recently, that horseshit about stem cell research growing new hands was a total nightmare. "But this?" it whimpered as its molecules were fired through a zip gun of light speed proportions. "How am I supposed to beat this?"

It sensed a red glow around its fringes. There was no one left to help.

Lloyd ran off minutes ago, leaving the hand to fend for itself. Things were looking grim and for the briefest of moments the hand wished it had been born a Robo-Mandible 2K, because maybe then it could at least crawl off.

"Please, Mister Black Hole," the hand said without fear or regret. "If you had any clue the shit I've been through." The hand briefly gazed into the dark expanse. "Hey, not so fast, don't forget, I'm partially responsible for getting you here," it said. While the hand didn't actually deduce quantum equations, or even write them down, it had picked up a fair amount of astrophysics in its forty or so years of being attached to Lloyd Caruthers.

The hand was popped from a rubber mold in a Chicago factory around 1969 and had survived those years to reach one crushing final conclusion. "You're just a thing. Just an item, just a noun," the hand sighed. "That son-of-a-bitch, mortality, will eat you alive. Some hands melt in house fires, some fall dead from heart attacks and some are astrophysically gnawed on by anomalies so powerful they suck in and traps matter, gas and light. That's not even mentioning the fact that their molecules are then ripped to such small shreds they wouldn't even amount to a pinch of salt."

The hand liked repeating some of the stuff it had learned about black holes and collapsing stars through the years.

The hand thought it was immortal until that moment it began disappearing. Then it felt really old and yet, like he'd hardly lived. The hand imagined that's what Veronique thought. Which was the last image on its mind as it shivered in the dark, waiting to step onto the third rail of existence.

NINE

"The oyster is your world."
-J. Claude Caruthers, *Nashville's Shakespeare*

The bus bounced off course, down some tiny state highway across the small of Tennessee's back. Morning sunlight fanned through the room while the greens and browns of dense tree cover buzzed past the window. The road was missing important chunks of pavement. The suspension springs groaned, but J. Claude ignored it. He ignored his cabinets and draws violently shaking open. He ignored everything but the voice hanging on the opposite end of the phone last night.

J. Claude was reminded of that careless time in the early eighties when his eyes stung from exhaustion this bad. While on a marathon tour of the United States and Canada, Shakespeare's bass player advised him to swallow a handful of speed and chug a bottle of cough medicine. Bassists are always full of homespun medicinal advice like that. The result was some detached purgatory where Caruthers wanted to sleep very badly, but his body was hotwired so his eyes wouldn't shut.

Still, that aching sleeplessness was nothing compared to his current state.

Since hanging up the phone, Claude's body clung to the mattress. He spent the night watching the ceiling tassels swing wild. After several hours, he lifted his arms and smelled the salty mix of last night's onstage sweat and tears. This was about the time a dab of inspirational cream poured into his anxietal coffee, and he dug out a dusty Casio keyboard from the closet.

All he accomplished was staring at its black and white keys because Caruthers' mind demanded sleep, but his tense body was nowhere near closing up shop. That gritty-voiced lady's promises of returning Rusty were enough to make Claude do a back flip. However, her other promises kept those eyes jammed wide open. She offered to return the thing J. Claude had been missing for so many years, the thing he lost once as a teenager and lost again in the summer of 1977.

These promises were a snake of nervous energy coiling around the musician and squeezing tighter. J. Claude's skeptical side didn't trust this mysterious voice. It all seemed too simple. Nobody gets their family back so easily. And for that matter, why'd she bring Denny Dynasty into all this?

Family was the one thing Claude had been aching for since his wife's death. Sold-out shows, adoring fans and hit records were a flimsy handshake compared to the full-bodied hug of family. He pretended to be estranged from Lloyd, but, in reality, the physicist ignored Claude's numerous attempts to reconnect.

When presented with the woman's raspy promise of a reunion, J. Claude battled an urge to phone his brother. Claude couldn't recall, but was pretty sure all his hair was in place when the twins last carried a conversation. After several false starts and hang-ups, Claude finally left a message on Lloyd's phone and tried the laboratory. Nobody answered. The singer thought that was funny, since it was probably early afternoon on a workday in Switzerland.

"Boss?" Judy didn't knock upon entering, her hair was a morning mess and pillow creases lined her face. She hadn't changed from pink wool pajamas. "I'm sorry to wake you."

"I'll bet."

"Look, we have to talk."

"Later. I got stuff on my mind."

"Skinny Richard won't turn the bus around."

"I said later and I meant it."

"He's heading in the wrong direction. We're going to be late for the next concert. Will you talk to him?"

Nashville's Shakespeare looked up, cross-legged on his bed with the electric keyboard in his lap. His face's seriousness was all the answer Judy needed. His normally tan, stiff features were drained and melted, the creature plinking digital notes resembled a Halloween getup. If exhaustion were a costume.

"No, I will not talk to Richard," he said and continued playing. He paused briefly and sniffed his nose before continuing. "The man has specific instructions."

Judy also snuffled at a sharp odor. It wasn't this bad yesterday, was it?

Neither realized an untouched club sandwich was wedged under Claude's bed, its creamy mayonnaise now the same shade of purple as the walls.

She ignored the stink and watched Claude's pale fingers knife into the piano. Judy gave a childish whine: "Claude, this is ridiculous and irresponsible. We need to be in Missoula tomorrow for your apology concert, remember? I have you booked on the AM radio station and local TV."

Judy pulled knotted hair apart waiting for his response. Claude's head hung above the Casio, silent and motionless. She mistakenly thought her boss had finally drifted off to sleep.

Claude's focus on the keys didn't break. "Because a man's got to do what a man's got to do." He played a few notes and looked at his publicist. His face softened, like maybe they shared similar pains. "Alright, you know when you have a few too many margaritas with dinner? You know how you start whining about missing your daddy?"

"Claude, this isn't appropriate. We are not talking about that." Her body grew noticeably rigid and distressed.

"Well, your family's only a phone call away."

"Conversation over, Claude."

"See, I always thought my family was separated by things a lot more dark and nasty than phone cables. But out of the blue, that call came in last night and I feel different. I feel like you, bitching and moaning and wishing things could be better with my family. Only difference is that I'm doing something about it instead of moping around, acting all lonely and sad." His face held the seriousness of a Supreme Court justice. J. Claude rolled up a sleeve. "Like I said in my book: The oyster is your world, man." He revealed a faded bicep tattoo of a clam shell circled by that self-quote. "Live it, Judy."

"This is the kind of thing," she thought, "even grumpy old Daddy would find laughable." Judy could melt the old man's black heart with some of her stories. Once, J. Claude tried burning down CBS headquarters because the station aired Kenny Rogers' popular *The Gambler* movie opposite J. Claude's Holiday Bonanza. But that snafu was mysteriously absent from *Nashville's Shakespeare.* Another time, at this concert in Portland, he kicked out every man in the audience who was taller than him. And that book certainly wouldn't mention the incident in Missoula last week. That kind of idiocy would undoubtedly fracture a nasty grin over Daddy's lips. That is, if he and Judy were still speaking.

"Well," her jaw was tight and her throat growled hoarse. The phantom scratching of tears was near. Judy desperately wanted the subject to change and didn't try stopping her trusted method. For years, she refused to act like her father in these situations. Using that psychology tied Judy's brain into knots when she was a girl. Normally, when the urge for such mumbo-jumbo came, she stomped off and downed a glass of wine instead. But her father's voice was strong when that sense of control slipped. The entire bus had the emptiness of death about it. Now she knew why. "If you want to ruin your career, go right ahead. You think fans were disappointed last night, just wait for Missoula. You'll never make anyone happy again."

"First of all, what happened in Missoula was self-defense."

J. Claude's chin touched his chest. His fingers tinkled high white keys.

"Self-defense? That woman was in her eighties. Her son walked with a cane. How can you call that self defe—"

Claude's voice chopped at the protest: "Secondly, they won't be disappointed. I'm writing the song. I'm making the oyster my damn world." His eyes shot up, bright, "You could learn a few things."

Her father's cruel voice disappeared, replaced by a thin ribbon of confusion, "Without Rusty?"

"It's coming slow, but I feel something. Listen, I can't explain what's happening in my head right now, it's a mess up there. But if giving Denny Dynasty a lift helps me get my family back together, I won't ever be concerned with fans again. I'll never need anyone's approval."

She stopped picking her hair.

He filled with a knowing grin and it ate at the publicist's guts.

"You're so selfish," Judy's voice sounded bloody. "I thought maybe I was helping you. But you're still a waste."

"What's that?" J. Claude's head turned away.

"I said—"

"What's that?"

"I said, you're a waste." She crossed her arms like it was the final word she'd ever speak.

"I'm sorry, I can't hear you, radio's too loud." He leaned over the bed, knocking the plastic keyboard to the floor, and flipped on his bedside stereo. The speaker came to life with an AM station. The disk jockey's voice was low and blank—the sound of tears squeezing from eyes.

This strange DJ stopped Judy and J. Claude's argument. Morning's sunlight fanned through the room.

The radioman said governments around the world were working on a solution, but advised citizens to stay calm. He reported the White House was urging people to refrain from calling it a "Black Hole." Instead, it was a, "colorless molecular disturbance." The American government had not ruled out the possibility of terrorism.

"What does that mean?" Judy's voice was vulnerable and damp. A punching built in her chest.

The singer fell back onto his bed, aching for sleep. "Nothing. Sounds a lot like scientific bullshit."

"How can you say that?"

"Because I hate science."

"I don't think this is a joke." She sat next to him and sank into the mattress. "This is scary."

A brutal lighting strike of fear quivered J. Claude's lip. But, like his twin, he was an ace at boxing up emotions and storing them in some dank warehouse. "Well, uhhh, my offer still stands to take off your dress. Maybe get your mind off things."

Judy lifted her chin and wet eyes. She gave a look that cramped Caruthers' stomach. Claude never actually thought Judy would stoop this low for sex—which was exactly why he hired her.

The radio report staggered on. J. Claude gulped and did his duty by inching closer. His temples throbbed with nervous blood. He asked Stella's forgiveness and reached a hand toward Judy's leg.

Their eyes connected—hers tired, his tired, hers wet, his something blank.

The publicist stood. Claude's heart went as blank as his eyes.

"Pig," she hissed and walked away.

The crooner fell back with relief and tried not to think about dying. Death had always been staring him down, but now it had a face and a smell. It was standing in the front row of the auditorium, waiting for him to finish the set, pointing at its wristwatch.

Judy hardened her expression and settled at the front of

the bus by the long bay window near the driver's seat. Had it really been eight years of working with this slimeball? Had it nearly been a decade since she turned down that job at Daddy's PR firm? She rubbed tired skin and blew hair from her eyes. How did a senior year internship evolve into this life?

Then she repeated the words that ferried her across similar oil-black days. "J. Claude needs me." Her head filled with helium and anger-numbing satisfaction.

After college, Judy was brought on to assist J. Claude's publicist at the time. Back then the redhead was fashionable, perky, thick-hipped with baby fat and brutally naïve. Reluctantly, she removed a beloved nose ring before starting the new job. Her hair was still the color of autumn leaves. The internship sounded like a blast, even though she had grown up on Long Island and hated country music. Who wouldn't spend a summer on a tour bus, zig-zagging the nation? Judy's main responsibility would be helping some has-been singer with his vowels and consonants. Nothing could be simpler.

Her internship went almost exactly according to plan, except one blindsided spin just before the tour of duty ended—the same day Judy was offered a name plaque on that corner office in New York City. J. Claude's original publicist was shaky and sleepless, constantly dealing with Caruthers' public relations bungles. The woman quit in Tulsa without a note or a call.

Judy had gotten to know J. Claude well, helping him mostly with fan mail and restaurant menus. She felt truly needed and it filled her head with joyful satisfaction. Growing up with a nanny, a tutor, a chef and two parents who hardly ever came home, Judy wasn't used to the weird sensation of being needed. Knowing someone's life would be much harder without her was a thrill. Sure, Caruthers pinched her butt and used that, "Take off your dress, stay awhile," line over and over. Sure, he constantly quoted his own autobiography, telling her: "If you put your mind to stuff, you can probably do it." But

Judy assumed she could add a little padding to her resume as
J. Claude's publicist. "Maybe," she thought, "end the pinching
and that tired pickup line. Craft him into a decent human being."

But now, if the news was true, the world was ending and a
frequently pinched bottom was all she had to show for it. After
all these years Claude's reading ability never improved and he
still used his pickup line.

Why had she invested so many sleepless nights mopping
up J. Claude's disasters? Like every other time she'd quizzed
herself, the answer came brutally fast. "Because nobody else
actually needs me."

The black fangs of doom were sinking in deep. "No time
to quit, Judy," she said, starting her laptop. She twisted her hair
into a ponytail, exhaled deep and stiffened into a business face.
"You have to tell that promoter in Missoula why J. Claude isn't
stopping by to apologize for shattering his jaw and kicking his
mother."

She sipped coffee and a tiny, delighted curl formed at her
lips.

"Do you hear this shit?" The bus driver, Skinny Richard,
called back to her, spinning the radio's volume knob. "This
black hole can't be stopped. It's creeping across the world, real
slow. We're all gonna die. We can't block it or plug it up. All of
Europe is just gone. Like MIA."

"I don't know, Richard. I don't honestly think anything is
going to happen." She slugged back more coffee. "Me, I'm
sending an email to Missoula, because that's what I would do if
there wasn't something over in Europe." Her voice was perky,
"because there probably isn't."

"Forget that. I'm living up the rest of my time. I'm going
to a strip club. I hope those dancers are as dumb as you and
still working."

She didn't even get to check an email before the bus lurched
to a stop. The Airstream was parked at a dingy truck stop with

a gentleman's club attached. "Take it easy," Richard hollered as he stepped from the bus. "Claude said to stop here, anyway. Supposed to pick someone up."

"Richard, no, you can't do this." She yelled but the only reply was the sound of commotion in the parking lot.

"That bastard," she heard a voice say. She turned to find Jesus rummaging through the cupboard. The chef was long and thin, wearing an Olympic Games T-shirt a dozen years past its prime. "I'm on your side. If the Lord wants us to die, I'm going to go out doing what I do best."

"That's a nice thought."

"There's a place in heaven for me. I'm sound."

"Really, there's no reason to panic."

"Who's panicked? I wish I was with my lady and kids, but that's life."

"I really don't know if this black hole is anything to worry about. It's like global warming. Is it really that dangerous?" Her face hung tired.

"What? So now you tell me you don't recycle either?"

"I'm just saying...nothing. I think Richard just quit. We're stuck."

"Stuck? No way. I used to pilot bigger buses than this before I was a cook. Let me show you." Jesus moved past Judy and hopped into the driver's seat.

"Really?"

He spent a few minutes showing her where the clutch was, how many gears the bus had and how an old model like this didn't include cruise control. "Man, it still has a choke switch. I don't even know what the hell that does. This baby's an antique."

He was showing Claude's publicist how to adjust the side mirrors when the door swung open and a wave of oily diesel fumes filled the cabin.

"Judy, long time no see," Denny Dynasty said, wearing too-tight jeans, a tanktop and a pink scarf. "You looked prettier in that cocktail dress last night." Using two fingers like tongs he picked up the Lifetime Achievement Award Caruthers had earned at the ceremony. Dynasty giggled like a toddler. "Where is the old maid? We have a lot of driving to do."

"We do?" She said, unenthused.

"Driver…" he sashayed to the front of the bus. "…garcon, to Memphis, *sill voos plate.*"

Jesus turned around, his ragged arms and faded black tattoos glowing in the windshield's sunlight. "Excuse me, miss?"

"I'm going to like you." Denny bent over with his hands on his knees, laughing. "And you're going to like me. Now turn this tub toward Memphis, pronto."

TEN

"Memphis has always been the leader of dirty work in the world."

   -J. Claude Caruthers, *Nashville's Shakespeare*[3]

"I do not appreciate this call," Lloyd spoke into his phone, arching his arm through the air, hoping the phantom pains would vanish. "I am trying to purchase a ticket to Montana and I do not have time for harassment."

LaGuardia Airport was a disaster of fists pounding countertops, screams weaving through rafters and the nervous, sweaty smell of thousands knowing death planned to swallow them whole soon.

The distraught travelers didn't know the squat, ponytailed man responsible for their panic. They didn't realize he was waiting for his turn at the Big Sky Airlines desk. There's no telling what they would have done, but it probably would have ended with Lloyd resembling a butcher shop's leftover bucket.

The afternoon sun fell powerfully through skylights, slicing shadows across the mob.

"Now, if you don't mind," Lloyd said, watching the grandmother at the front of the line walk away with a ticket. "I have to be going."

"He's not there," the woman's voice said. It was scratchy and dry. "Your brother won't be in Missoula today. Not that

---

3 Upon further research, the author discovered this was actually first spoken by blues singer "Sleepy" John Estes.

he'd live long enough to ever go back."

"My…" Confusion swelled his head more than when he had abandoned Veronique. More painful and reluctant than running from the Hadron lab without warning coworkers. His skull stung harder than during his nine hour flight across the Atlantic, realizing poor Karen, his promising assistant, was dead. "Brother? How do you know I have a brother?"

"I guess you'd only recognize my handwriting, not my voice." The woman's words were slammed together, impatient. "It's me, Zygmut."

A shock threw off his balance and Lloyd dug a knee into carpet. His mouth was suddenly flavored with blood. "My sister is dead. Goodbye."

"I'm not dead, Cubby. I know you read my letters. Now pull it together, you're too smart to play dumb." Sweat built behind his ears, he hadn't been called Cubby in decades. "Change planes, come to Memphis."

An instinct itched to inform this woman he hadn't been home since graduation and didn't plan on starting now. But the physicist froze. For the second time in twenty-four hours, Lloyd's stiffness resulted in losing someone. Luckily, this time it was only this woman as the phone connection fizzled out.

Emotions were uncovered inside him like from some dusty museum piece and Lloyd panicked at the ticket desk. Until a few hours ago, Lloyd despised his twin and couldn't have been paid enough to see Claude. But that *New York Times* article changed the color of their relationship.

Even walking through LaGuardia, Caruthers didn't know why he chose New York. His initial instinct was to be as far away from the black hole as possible. Why he didn't book a flight to Japan or Australia, he couldn't say. The Geneva to New York flight was the earliest, which didn't hurt.

On that trans-Atlantic plane, Lloyd spotted a front page story in the Arts and Entertainment section about a disastrous Country Music Awards the previous night. Apparently, J.

Claude made some promise to end his ridiculous songwriting project that evening. The sight of his brother's name caused the physicist to crumple the paper. But the enormous three-column photo of J. Claude—dropped to his knees on the stage with tears running down his face—made Lloyd continue reading. Some charred blackness deep inside actually hummed with pleasure, seeing his brother cry.

According to the report, the crowd expected him to sing a song named after their sister. Apparently, J. Claude never finished the tune. Reading those lines thawed Lloyd's icicle attitude. "Of course Claude couldn't write a song about Zygmut," the physicist thought, "that'd just about kill him."

Standing onstage with Kenny Rogers and some sparkly kid named Denny Dynasty, Nashville's Shakespeare buckled. According to the report, Claude only mumbled a few lyrics, which were reprinted in a sidebar.

Zygmut
Oh Ziggy
Oh, where did you go?
You stupid bitch
I'll never know
You left me and Lloyd and that was pretty shitty in my opinion
And for that matter, what about mom and dad? Where the hell did they go?
We were sixteen for god's sake, that ain't right. I mean, at least leave a note or something. Thank god Lloyd got that scholarship to Yale, because he'd be worse off than me, probably deejaying at a strip club or something. But he showed you, didn't he? Lloyd didn't need you to be great. But me, come on, this shit's been killing me for, like, years…

The audience reportedly began shouting insults and hurling snakeskin boots until Kenny Rogers and Dynasty jumped into a duet, singing The Gambler. The kid was a hit, really hamming it up and the *Times* critic hailed it as, "Denny Dynasty's coming out party, and we're not talking about the closet." The music writer also briefly noted how this *Dynasty* fella looked very perky without eyelashes.

The article pushed and bullied a brotherly fire within Lloyd. It was one thing to hate your twin, but when an entire auditorium booed, his mouth got dry and fingernails latched the armrest. The urge for a reunion grew inside the multiple-PhD holder. Its pace was almost as omnivorous as his desire to be remembered. Both chomped away at the pie-eating contest of Lloyd's soul.

The article said J. Claude's next performance was some apology concert in Missoula for assaulting an old lady and her son. In Lloyd's estimation, this would give the brothers a few minutes before the black hole caught up.

Death was inevitable and the scientist wanted to be by Claude's side, friends again, when it happened.

Standing in front of Big Sky Airline's desk—the ticket agent's face growing red and angry behind her tasteful blue suit—Lloyd still waivered.

"My sister says to go to Memphis," he mumbled in the same hushed rant J. Claude utilized on the award show stage. "But the newspaper says Missoula. I don't know what to do."

"Pardon me? Sir, people are desperate to get out of here."

"I can't decide."

"Tell me specifically what you want. That thing is coming and I need to get my jewelry out of my apartment after this shift, so if you could speed this up."

"Memphis or Missoula, which would you choose?" His voice lifted slightly as the hustle and hammer of a thousand frightened airport voices faded. "That can't really be my sister, can it?"

Lloyd visualized the three photos in his bag. He scooped them up on his way out of the laboratory. He wanted to line up Einstein, Oppenheimer and Hawking for their opinion. Lloyd wanted a scholarly approach. But the queue began erupting and Lloyd knew he didn't have time for consultation.

The woman tapped a few lines into her computer and tilted an impatient head. "Missoula's sold out, hun. There's one seat left for Memphis. But honestly, I wouldn't want to die in Memphis. You ever been there? Kind of yuck, if you know what I mean."

That relief, the freedom from choosing, lifted Lloyd from his shoes. "I'll take it. One for Memphis," he smiled briefly, but then focused on the ball of guilty invisible fire building where his hand used to be.

ELEVEN

"Look at me, ladies and gentlemen! I'm living like a burst of fireworks."

-J. Claude Caruthers, *Nashville's Shakespeare*

The Club Sandwich coughed and groaned. Trapped far under that dark bed—with her lettuce wilted to brown vellum, her turkey yellow and sweatsock pungent between three layers of tough, mold-speckled bread—she prayed for death.

"Please, someone, notice me. Throw me away." Every savory inch of the sandwich hurt, but her feelings were damaged worst. She'd slid from the floor to her current location a few weeks prior when that jackass bus took a sharp turn in Pittsburgh.

J. Claude never once clamped teeth into her. Not even his customary nibble. The sandwich knew when Jesus began assembling her ingredients that she had one mission. The Club never felt more alive than when she knew this world had a purpose. She always pictured herself lying proudly among the other plates with one large chomp carved from her body. J. Claude only ever took single bites from sandwiches, which she considered a brilliant artistic statement.

"Nothing ever tastes as good as your first sip of beer or your first bite of a sandwich," Claude proudly quoted from his book whenever Judy got on his case about starving kids in Africa. "After that, it's all repetition. I'm living like a burst of fireworks. I want my whole life to be that first, full bite. I want all the flavor, baby. Now why don't you remove your dress and let me have a taste?"

"I'm wearing slacks," was all the sandwich heard Judy say before she stormed off.

Under the bed, long forgotten cigarettes rolled across the floor as she knocked into guitar picks and worn boots. Thinking about her premature demise made the Club weep.

The sandwich wanted to bring Claude joy. She felt a kinship with the singer, knowing they both specialized in creating happiness. She'd heard J. Claude remark that, "smiling was illegal until I was sixteen. My parents refused to allow smiling or laughing or fun of any kind. The happiest day of my life came when I was orphaned. That was my first taste of fun. Now I'm just spreading that joyful first bite in everything I do."

The grim bus felt eerily similar to J. Claude's childhood stories and it made the sandwich ache with loneliness. There weren't many smiles on board. Lately, Judy would bicker about something professional and Claude would wince in his seclusion, either about missing Stella or not being able to write that final song. "You ever thought about how we're all gonna die and nobody'll remember us? They remember the Julius Caesars and the Ghandis, but who was the J. Claude Caruthers of two hundred years ago? Who was the equivalent of you? Nobody remembers."

The sandwich also wanted to leave a delicious legacy, but now her life was coming to an end. She knew all those scrumptious ingredients were wasted.

"Wasn't I special enough? Why was I forgotten?" the Club asked, realizing her dehydrated and shriveled tomato resembled J. Claude's complexion. "I had one job on this planet and I blew it. Now what's left?"

All morning the Club Sandwich listened to J. Claude and Judy discuss this black hole business. Later, the sandwich forgot her painful troubles at the amusing sound of Nashville's Shakespeare barring Dynasty from the bedroom. The sandwich liked how miserable Judy was, passing messages between both stars. The publicist deserved it for making J. Claude so sad all the time and for not putting the Club Sandwich out of her misery by cleaning under the bed.

"Tell that little girl to return my guitar," J. Claude screamed from beneath his purple sheets.

"Dynasty says he didn't take Rusty. I believe him." The sandwich saw Judy's smooth knees drop to the carpet, she lowered her head to the floor, sniffing. "You saw Denny run away when the Caruthers' Kids got loose. He didn't have your guitar." The sandwich sensed the publicist getting closer. "God, what is that smell?"

"Someone's got Rusty. I want him back." The Club felt J. Claude pound a fist on the mattress and capture Judy's attention. "I need Rusty back. I have to finish this thing before the thing gobbles me up. This piano sounds worse than Dynasty's voice. I can't write a song without my guitar."

"Claude, there are more important things to think about." Judy's knees were off the floor as she impatiently tapped a toe.

"Nothing's more important than being remembered. Nothing's more important than me finishing this song, Judy. Quit being stupid."

"Don't you dare talk to me like that. I am so fed up with your shit." Her feet turned toward the main cabin of the bus. "Hey, Denny, how many people are going to be around when we get sucked up by the black hole?"

"Colorless molecular disturbance, sweetie. Call a spade a spade." The Club Sandwich heard Dynasty walk toward the back of the bus. "No sudden moves, Claude. I got my eye on you."

The sandwich sensed a tension in the stale air. She knew the two men were watching each other, maybe a moment from gouging eyes and trading fists.

"But to answer your question," Denny regained his flamboyance. "None. Nobody will give a shit about country music once we're ripped into a million strings of spaghetti."

Silence and confusion followed.

"What? Don't make those faces at moi," Denny said. I have a Master's in Particle Physics from Vanderbilt. I just started singing to put myself through school. Theorists say once you pass the event horizon, every fiber of your body is pulled into strands of spaghetti. Read a book, folks."

Judy's condescending voice rose to the purple tassels. "See? You aren't the most important person on Earth and this song doesn't matter. We're all going to die and there won't be anyone left to remember you."

The Club didn't sense any movement. But she heard Claude sit up, something weak and sad filtered through his throat. "Can I be honest with you all? If none of this stuff matters, what am I supposed to do?"

Judy shifted into something stunned: "I don't know. I don't know what anyone is supposed to do."

"Oh, since we're playing question and answer," Dynasty always spoke as if he were MCing a child's birthday, even in the face of doom. "How much longer until we reach Memphis? I have to pee and I've seen ditches more sanitary than this toilet."

The Airstream jerked forward. Denny's body beat into the wall. The sound and vibration of grinding gears found the sandwich. She was glad she hadn't died yet, this stuff was finally getting interesting.

"You shut your mouth," Claude sounded rough. The sandwich heard a cigarette lighter snap to life above her. "That bathroom has worked beautifully for thirty years. You would be so lucky to take a leak on this bus."

"Whatever," Dynasty said.

"Speaking of Memphis," Judy was back to normal. "Why are we going there, of all places?"

Denny now sounded pale and uninterested. "Beats me. It's

just what Dirt Clod Caruthers' sister told me to do. She gave me an address and the whole works."

"Dynasty, my sister is dead." Claude's voice fizzled down to a shaky whimper. "I think… Now you just shut your mouth."

"Whatever, old man. You know I'm right or we'd be heading to some shitburg like Missoula right now."

"Denny," Claude said with a sharpness. "Shut up. I have bigger problems. I need to write this song."

"Here's a better question," Denny announced with the voice of a disgusted teenage girl. "What is that awful smell back here?"

TWELVE

"Family's where it's at. A man crosses his family, might as well carve himself a tombstone…that sonbitch is dead, from the inside out."

-J. Claude Caruthers, *Nashville's Shakespeare*

"Okay, this crap isn't fun anymore," the former proton thought.

Since colliding with his wife, Audrey, Mister Proton was rapidly spreading and the initial thrill of being a black hole wore off quickly. The rush of power reminded him of movies where a stick of dynamite is lit. Wick turns to ash and tension builds in your gut waiting for the big pop. Well, as Mr. Proton grew bigger and stronger, he felt a redeeming tension at his center, or Event Horizon in terms Lloyd and Denny would understand. Screams of terror in a hundred different languages disintegrated to dust and sent a happy chill through him. Sucking in shimmering beams of light, the smells of fresh patisserie bread and the entire German Black Forest, gobbling humans and buildings and cars and computers by the ton seemed like the perfect revenge at first.

Clearly, the only way to make up for the loss of his wife and family was through bloodlessly efficient destruction.

"Oh, no, no," he worried now. A shameful quivering rocked his core. "I'm sorry, I can't stop myself." The colorless molecular disturbance sounded raw and panicked as its borders spread wider. A pitch black ripple on an oily dark pond. He brought all of Barcelona into his grip and thought about the eerie silence within.

The world's carnival of color and action crash-stopped when it touched the darkness. He was the Grim Reaper on autopilot. Spain, for some reason, reminded Mister Proton of his children.

"Someday, if you kids study hard," he once noted during tuck-in time. "You can be whatever you want. Along with the billions of other protons out there, we make the world. Atom-by-atom, you and you and you and you," he said, kissing each of his proton children on the forehead, "are the most important things on the planet. Without us, there'd be nothing."

"I want to be part of a Formula One racecar," his oldest boy said.

"I'm going to be a beautiful silk dress," his daughter said.

"I'm going to be a football player's cleat, the right one, the one that kicks all the goals," the middle boy said.

"And what about you, bub?" he asked the baby.

"I want to be a plate of tapas," he exclaimed. The youngest was infatuated with his Spanish lessons.

The black hole's heart ached, thinking of all the tapas bars converted to sooty, silent nothingness. He'd swallowed his children and wife whole. His bowling team was gone, his postman, his parents. Everyone. That selfish sweep of power and revenge ruined everything. Not to mention himself.

It took molecular cannibalism to realize that's all life was, just those silly connections. Eating and talking and meeting different people and trying new things were the keys to happiness. And really, what else was there?

A deep sobbing began as his border touched the Atlantic Ocean, unable to stop.

"I'll never have another one of those connections," he thought and tried with all his might to reverse course, to collapse and swallow himself. He'd heard that scientist, Caruthers, talk about a similar theory. Nobody was too worried about black holes to begin with, since the scientific community assumed they'd fizzle out and collapse. "Well, if things get too hairy," Lloyd once joked to a doomsday protestor outside the Hadron Collider's gate, "I'll just whip up a white hole, boom, counteract the whole shebang."

The black hole tightened its gut and pushed inward with everything—which was substantial, considering he'd just turned a quarter of the planet to intergalactic dust—but nothing changed. He didn't have the inner strength to create a white hole and collapse.

The black hole was on a collision course with North America.

THIRTEEN

"This one time, I told Kenny Rogers: Sorry's just another thing that don't mean shit."
  -J. Claude Caruthers, *Nashville's Shakespeare*

Claude's bedroom door was open. Judy and Denny watched with confusion as he drifted into suffocating sleep. Nashville's Shakespeare soon jerked from those warm dreams and comfort. "You can't knock off now," he muttered. "Keep singing, keep writing, can't stop. What would she say to you?"

"She? Is he talking about you?" Denny whispered and wrinkled his princess-shaped nose at the smell of the engine burning oil. Jesus had really screwed up something as he got reacquainted with bus driving. The motor coach was outside Memphis, but still on back roads. Tree branches scraped the aluminum sides like enormous claws. Stacked dinnerware clattered together over each bump.

"I doubt it. I don't know who he's talking about. Claude hasn't slept in about two weeks," she faced Dynasty, eyes nothing more than exhausted smears.

"He looks it."

"It's my fault. Before the Awards, I made him stay up to write that song, but now I don't think it's healthy for someone his age. He could be hallucinating and talking to the Queen of England at this point."

The she J. Claude muttered about became clear when the singer began playing an elaborate game of patty-cake, making

82

a jazzy drum skin of flesh and pantlegs. The voice accompanying the beat—even though Claude shuddered with insomnia and death—was smooth and golden again.

Stella, my lovely, Ohhhhhhh, Stella
Lean back, you beauty, let me tell ya
This man's never seen a sight more thrilling
Nor felt such a natural high
As seeing the world's most beautiful girl
Jump a motorcycle through the sky
Jump a motorcycle through the sky

The singer's face pinched. J. Claude took dry, desert island gasps. His nerves were cooling from nuclear meltdown to something far less radioactive. Singing the only one of his twenty-one hundred songs that meant a damn thing always soothed Caruthers' anxiety.

But a lonesome ache still echoed up his chest without Rusty's accompaniment.

Caruthers' eyelids were plump and heavy, purple with bloated skin. They frequently slammed shut like loose windows, but he always jerked back to life. Claude had been playing this game for at least an hour. Bridging bouts of sleep and explosions of waking, he pushed around what Denny and Judy said.

Were his songs worthless? Does it matter if anyone remembers you?

Normally, Claude was a master at neglecting his sorrow. Submarine designers never built anything as watertight as J. Claude's emotional core. But Judy and Denny were right and it raked hot coals over that sadness. Claude was going to die. Nothing would soothe the salt gritting up these cuts.

The bus made a violent jerk and the dinner plates tinkled. "We're here," Jesus called.

"Where's here?" the singer hollered down to the front of

the bus. J. Claude, staggering toward the chef, was blinded by white evening light flooding through the enormous windshield.

"Beats me. Ask your little buddy." Jesus cleared nasal passages.

"Beats me," Denny said, adjusting the dainty pink scarf around his fleshy neck. "I was just told to deliver Captain Crybaby. Zygmut never said anything but the address."

"You shut up, Denny," J. Claude stared Dynasty down. In his bare feet, Caruthers was shocked to learn Denny was an inch or two taller. Claude pinched his lips until they stung. He could tolerate smart alecs, but tall people turned his lungs to Agent Orange. "I'll let you drown in my tears. You don't know what kind of stress I'm under."

"No, no, there's nothing wrong with crying," Dynasty slid into an evil grin. "It's just a little feminine, don't you think?" Denny's womanly voice could have doubled for Jane Jetson's.

All thoughts of songwriting and patching together families disappeared with a hot rage squealing tires across J. Claude's heart. "Get me out of here. I need some air." He shoved the lanky singer aside and burst out the door.

A gust of sharp pine, along with something moist and rotten, blew into the bus as Judy, Denny and Jesus traded uneasy glances.

The landscape outside the bus was an acre or so of overgrown lawn fenced in on all sides by bushy fir trees tug-o-warring with the breeze. A few hundred feet away, standing high above the brown and green thickets, was a house. A simple Cape Cod with its central window holding steady above a sagging porch. Scraps of pristine white paint hung to the sides, but mostly it was peeled and scraped down to a decayed grey. The trim was once minty green, but had tarnished into something organically dark.

"Well I'll be damned," J. Claude's voice was stunned. He shuffled bare feet through painful gravel and red Memphis dirt.

To him, the house didn't look condemned. Caruthers didn't notice the moss splotching the roof or the shattered windows. In his eyes, it was as bright and welcoming as it was in 1962.

"What is this place?" Judy said, stepping from the bus and shading her eyes. Frail bugs landed on milky city-girl skin and stung, even as she swatted.

"Whoa," Denny poked his head from the bus. His moussed hair glimmered in the sun and attracted a swarm of black insects. "So we're stopping at a haunted house?"

"No, asshole," J. Claude's voice was creamy, full of wonder. "It's my home. I grew up here."

J. Claude's childhood was curiously absent from his autobiography. Everything before his lonely hitchhiked journey to Nashville with nothing but a guitar and guilt on his back, was unknown to the public. Even the year of his birth was disputed. Some researches claimed the tiny country legend was fifty-six years old, while others went as low as forty-nine.

"You lived here?" Judy said, spinning around, absorbing the tranquil surroundings. The gentle bird calls and leafy tree hiss cooled her doomed concerns.

"Where are your parents?" Denny said, almost like he hadn't heard the rumors around Music Row. Again, this guy played the lead in *Mame*, he was a hell of an actor.

Claude rubbed his stubble, stunned. "Dead, I suppose. Maybe not. I thought you'd know, Denny."

"Look, I have reasons for coming here, but enlightening you on mammy and pappy ain't one of them." He made a skeptical twist where his eyebrows were plucked. "Remind me, were they first or second cousins?"

"I'll dig your grave in this yard if you don't take that back." Claude's face burned red, his hands were greased in sweat. They reached out for a fistful of Dynasty's scarf. "My parents were loving, fine people. Raised me right. Went to church every Sunday." Claude eased his grip and pink silk slipped through fingers. "At least they did until I was twelve."

Denny's face was unconcerned. He blotted a sweaty forehead with the scarf's end.

"Claude?" Judy moved toward her boss, recognizing a strange color in his voice: something nostalgic and sad, the tone he used when recalling good times with Stella. A womanly instinct crawled from the darkness and took control. Wrapping a tender arm around Caruthers, Judy felt him opening. She didn't doubt for a moment it would happen. The rewarding lump in her throat matched, beat and easily decapitated those long-forgotten thrills of helping J. Claude sound out restaurant menus. "J. Claude needs me," she reminded herself.

"Honest, not much to report before then. We were a happy little family. My dad was a veteran, served on a destroyer in the South Pacific, helped sink a Japanese fleet. Mom stayed home with us. Me and my brother pretended to be Daniel Boone and my sister listened to Patsy Cline records, talked on the phone all day.

"But man, when me and Lloyd were twelve..." his sound drizzled. "Look, we stopped getting dressed up early on Sunday mornings to go to St. Agnes. Instead, my parents and sister barely ever rolled out of bed before noon, even on weekdays. Dad quit as foreman at the slaughterhouse. Those three'd go off somewhere every night. Late. Left me and Lloyd to fend for ourselves. All the kids at school said they joined a cult, which wasn't something people talked about in those days. But nobody talked about nothing at our house. You ask 'em where they were last night and they said something just to shut us up, 'Oh, at the library.' 'At the grocery store.' 'Volunteering at the soup kitchen.'

"But we knew that wasn't true. Eventually they lost their interest in me and Lloyd. We cooked for ourselves, mowed the lawn, washed our clothes. Mom and dad didn't care if my brother and I lived or died, let alone school, so I dropped out. Hated it, anyhow. Lloyd ran in the other direction, all he ever did was school. Mrs. Rankin would always boot him from the library at closing time."

Dynasty pretended not to hear, but quick side glances told J. Claude where the rival singer's head was.

Judy's sympathy warmed and she clutched her boss tighter. She didn't know anyone had suffered childhood neglect like her. J. Claude's story was even rougher than her own. A deep, sad pang twisted through her organs for Lloyd Caruthers, too. Suddenly, she felt fortunate to know her parents were alive. She determined to call them soon.

"Me, I just got a job washing beer mugs at a honky-tonk. Learned to pick a guitar. So, I guess, my folks doing what they did made us the men we are."

The group walked through a narrow gap in the weeds toward the porch while Claude spoke. The stalks and thistles swung back and forth across a concrete path that once sliced through the yard.

"One night, when we were sixteen, they just didn't come back. I guess mom and dad and Ziggy ran away to be Jehovah's Witnesses or Moonies or whatever. A few weeks later, Lloyd was finishing up his science fair project in the back room and I was helping." Claude's voice changed from matter-of-fact to something darker. "That's when he lost his hand. Thanks to me. Needless to say, I booked it toward Nashville not long after."

The three stood on the porch when he finished. The floorboards were rotten with holes and animal nests. Denny held his face to a dirty window while Judy's instincts said to rub Claude's shoulders. "I'm so sorry," she whispered. A vision appeared: Claude's twin brother on the cover of the newspaper, standing next to the collider, looking as excited as a pallbearer. "Now," she thought, "I know why Lloyd looked so sad on the happiest day of his life. That poor, poor man."

"Well," Claude said, quickly snapping back to that gruff voice—the one constantly bossing Judy around. "Lot of good sorry does us when we're going to die any minute. Lot of good it does when our legacy's swallowed by darkness. Just like that bus or my guitar," he sighed. "Sorry's just another thing that don't mean shit."

Surrounded by tender and painful nostalgia, a burning spread inside Claude. His song and his legacy were just things, too. "Things don't mean shit," he thought. "Not when you're dead." And at that moment, the barre chords and musical notes within his songwriting brain compacted and crumpled until they were set free with instructions never to return. "I don't want to write another song," he thought. "What good'll it do?"

Denny jangled the doorknob with no success and walked to the other end of the porch. Acting restless or nervous, he kept moving. The only time Dynasty stopped was to squeak open a corroded mailbox. "Well, look at what we have here."

"Huh?" Judy took a step in his direction and felt the floorboards bow.

"Don't touch my shit, Denny," Claude whined.

"Who, me?"

"Mail tampering's a federal offense," he said. "Spend the next five years…forget it."

Denny slipped out a crisp white envelope, the color of the house paint in J. Claude's memory.

"Don't be an ass. That's mine."

"Someone's the middle child."

"I'm the youngest by a couple minutes, genius." Claude held the envelope for a moment and smelled its pulpy newness. He squinted and lifted it to the light without a word. He turned the envelope over a few times and made a blank stare at the smudgy address.

After a moment of inspection, Judy snatched it from between Claude's fingers. "It's addressed to you and Lloyd."

Fourteen

"I've been waiting my whole life to be immortal."
-J. Claude Caruthers, *Nashville's Shakespeare*

The past twenty-four hours had knotted the world. When Lloyd boarded in Geneva—before news spread of some creeping global shadow swallowing lives without prejudice—travelers behaved normally. Everyone was busy with serious places to go, shoving and hustling through the plane's cabin and into the airport only to shove and hustle at the baggage claim. The world's frantic pace, Lloyd thought, was almost fast enough to match two light speed protons in a drag race. But, he thought with a stiff frown, no matter how fast we live our lives, we'll never outlive life.

Deplaning in Memphis, Lloyd realized the entire planet must have come to terms with his horrible experiment. Reactions had tamed since New York. Passengers were not rushed and had no place to go. Everyone was sluggish and quiet through the 757, all the way to the luggage carousel. Memphis International was so silent the prerecorded security announcements boomed with rock concert force. Each syllable agitated uncertain waters within the crowd. The world was going through the stages of grieving—in New York everyone was angry, but a few hours later they were contemplative. People seemed to have collectively moved on from rage to whatever this was.

Lloyd didn't have any luggage. His briefcase held yesterday's *New York Times* and three framed photos. He felt the other passengers were more noble. "How do you pack for death?" he thought, rising up the escalator. He admired the clueless children playing and babbling. Lloyd envied their ignorance of dying. "How would Oppenheimer pack?"

Lloyd checked his phone and became overwhelmed in punishing thoughts. Zygmut had left a message and said to come home.

Where had she been hiding? Why call now? Sure, there were those crazy letters, but Lloyd half-assumed it was some practical joke. Didn't he?

Zygmut's mention of their childhood house—that cheerful little Cape Cod where he once inhaled honeysuckle and squeezed the flowers for droplets of sweetness—attracted a swarm of memories.

He signaled a taxi and realized that, along with memories, the phantom pains had returned. His absent fingers were now five long nails driving into his wrist, each red hot and forged from guilt. That rubber hand effectively blocked his mind from remembering that day, at age sixteen, when he lost everything. Maybe Memphis brought it out? But now, equal parts nauseous and nostalgic, he recalled that moment Claude assisted with the chemistry set. The memory was so vivid, a shiver choked his spine.

Mom and Dad were always so perfect, so balanced, when he was little. They finished each other's sentences and gave little cheek kisses for no reason.

This stopped being Lloyd's worry, though, when Mom and Pop began speaking in whispers around the house and staying up late at night. They stopped giving the twins hugs. By the time he was sixteen, lying by himself in the hospital without a hand, Lloyd assumed even the most perfect love faded. If it happened to Mom and Dad, how could he expect better?

Thus began life's tangled foxtrot with romance—equally nuzzling it and shoving it down flights of stairs. Somewhere in this scrum, his new desire for immortality spread further and swallowed more real estate. Since watching his chances of a family disappear in a red flash at the Hadron lab, this desire's alarm clock rang heavy.

Maybe Zygmut was a little responsible for Lloyd's commitment phobia, too. She and Lloyd were best friends growing up, even though she was past kindergarten when he was born. Big Sister helped the curious boy with math and science—classes she excelled at. In return, he drew the girl pictures and played the bad guy when she and her friends pretended to be cowgirls. Lloyd's urge to be the hero in white nearly brought him to tears each time, but little Lloyd kept up the game for Zygmut. When she started following her parents' path to midnight secrecy, Lloyd fell into a reclusive role not unlike Claude's. As the forgotten family crumbs, the twins formed a distant, foggy bond.

When Lloyd shook from this memory, Memphis' dilapidated streets were zipping by the taxi window. Buildings and signs unpainted for decades, roads long forgotten and overflowing barrels of garbage formed a crushing landscape. An invisible force pressed his chest tight. Something forgotten dangled from his eye. He hadn't cried since acting as a cowgirl's villain.

"I guess I'm the bad guy again," he thought with a sigh as the cab driver's radio spoke of a deadly mystery crippling the planet. Lloyd was the man in black, pulling out a sidearm and shooting the world in the back from a Swiss laboratory. "That's what the books'll say, if anyone remembers." Caruthers cracked open the briefcase and ran a finger over cold framed shots of his three idols, "sorry to let you down, fellas."

"Un-frickin'-believable," the driver said with a sober tone, dodging through traffic.

"What?" Lloyd snuffled and cleared his eyes.

"This colorless molecular disturbance, this is how it ends? Un-frickin'-believable."

"Suppose so," Lloyd recognized the path through Memphis' streets toward the house. The city still looked like 1971. The barbecue restaurants had changed names, but the buildings still stood firm, like a perfect physics equation. "Sir, out of curiosity, why are you still working if you know it's the end?"

"I don't know. Maybe I hoped it'd take my mind off things. You know, make a couple of bucks in case."

"In case what?"

"In case this is all a hoax."

Lloyd recognized the man's step in the grieving process. He went through the same terrors when his parents, sister and brother deserted him at sixteen. Faced with an awful truth, Lloyd denied anything happened. It took the intervention of a hospital psychologist to convince the teenager his hand wasn't growing back. And for a moment, watching Veronique's innocent face stretch into a frightened howl, he decided it was a trick of light. Denial choked reality until Lloyd stepped into the Swiss night and realized he and Veronique would never share that air again.

"Don't tell yourself it's not real," Lloyd said, wrapping his left hand over the smooth stump. "Denying something scary exists only makes it worse."

"Thanks, Doctor Phil," the driver made an evil squint in the rearview. His horn beeped and he jerked the taxi around a slower car.

Lloyd fought the urge to argue, smack a palm on the shatterproof glass and say the cabbie was ungrateful. But the astrophysicist took a breath and remembered who was responsible for this mess.

Would there be a black hole if Team Orange ended up going first? And, for a beat, Lloyd blamed his sister, or whoever kept sending those odd letters. If that note hadn't suggested food poisoning, if it hadn't told him how to spread botulism, he wouldn't have been the Neil Armstrong of Big Bangs.

His tight chest grew hot and limbs buzzed with numbness imagining millions of people dying because he tainted the Orange Team's lunch. Because he flipped a switch to smash those protons together.

"I was always so upset my experiments only raised more questions," he thought. "Science closed a door and nature demolished all the windows." A grim chuckle left his lips. "The old way doesn't sound so bad anymore."

Only the car's engine made a noise as Memphis traffic congestion thinned into the thick green trees of the city's outskirts. Lloyd clutched his stump tight in the cab's silent stress.

Turning down a long gravel driveway, Lloyd was struck with an idea as brilliantly obvious as when he figured out how to recreate the Big Bang. "I would live on forever," he remembered, hell, be celebrated, "if I just reversed everything. Maybe instead of nature opening the windows, I could do the job."

The sunset sky above the tree line was navy and orange as the exhausted Cape Cod shrugged into view. The memory of the house was a blinding blur, not unlike Oppenheimer's first atomic test.

"White hole," Lloyd whispered.

"Huh?" The cabbie said, pulling next to a purple bus Lloyd hadn't even noticed. He never noticed anything when his mind was deep inside a physics tornado.

"The opposite of a black hole. Pushes matter away, instead of sucking it in."

"Well, I can't say this hasn't been interesting. It'll be thirty-eight bucks."

Lloyd handed him fifty and stepped from the cab, numbers and complex equations tickertaping through his head. Scientifically, the idea of black hole reversals occupied some laughable corner of study reserved for the California Mystery House and Scottish lake monsters. But that suddenly didn't concern him.

The physicist walked between weeds, down a cracked concrete pathway, as if he were fifteen and simply returning from school.

Lloyd didn't stop factoring until his foot made the porch

boards crackle and a voice called.

"Oh wow," a woman with stunning red hair said. "You have to be Lloyd."

"Pardon?"

"Nobody else could look that much like Claude."

"Cubby? What are you doing here?" His brother, J. Claude, wrapped two tight arms around the physicist, ruining his train of thought.

FIFTEEN

"Correct me if I'm wrong, but wasn't it the great Jimmie Rodgers who said, 'Drinking and playing guitar is like eating a pig. You better start with the heart or you're screwed.'"
  -J. Claude Caruthers, *Nashville's Shakespeare*[4]

Rusty's strings still vibrated. Even though he'd been locked in the blackness of a guitar case for hours, he relived this new-found freedom with glee and guilt.

For a short while, the Country Music Awards after-party was the battered guitar's crowning moment. The actual party was painfully dull at first: executives and millionaires swallowing oysters Rockefeller and sipping bubbly wine. But after a few snooty hours, one singer opened a case of bourbon in the storage room and a who's-who of country legends held a secret sing-along to escape high-falootin' boredom.

That tight room was stacked to the ceiling with Costco containers of olive oil, paprika, wild rice and everything else fancy restaurants keep on hand.

By some miracle, Rusty ended up being the only musical instrument present. The guitar was passed from star-to-star.

Under a dim fifty-watt bulb, the group harmonized and hollered. The classic tunes were strummed and Rusty never knew life was so vibrant. Some were fingerpickers, some formed chords with nimble hands, some slid an empty whis-

---

4 This quote, oddly enough, was not originally attributed to Jimmie Rodgers, but J. Claude Caruthers.

key bottle over frets to play blues, one fella from a bluegrass group even plucked Rusty like a banjo. Each branded a special new memory into his maple body. It'd been decades since anyone but J. Claude Caruthers played the guitar. That night, little Rusty was the last filet mignon tossed into a hungry lion cage and he loved it.

Hank Williams, Johnny Cash, Merle Haggard, Earnest Tubb—all the classic songs were in heavy rotation that night. However, the songs of J. Claude Caruthers didn't make an appearance. No Devilish Deidra, no Cryin' for Margot, no Naomi Fever—nothing from Caruthers' catalog.

Long after the jam session ended, in total darkness, Rusty's spirits dropped down to Earth upon inspecting his surroundings. The guitar case was black and quiet. "This might as well be my coffin," he thought. "Compared to last night, everything is just a step closer to dying."

Toward the end of the evening, the festive spirit unraveled in drunkenness and fatigue. With the sun nearly up and the collection of singers rapidly dwindling, Rusty was exhausted from working hard not to break a string. "This is, by far, the best guitar I have ever played," Denny Dynasty commented. He strummed some sweet chords and plucked a stunning blues riff. "Kenny, I can't thank you enough."

"For stealing J. Claude's guitar?" A chuckle bounced from Kenny Rogers' dove-colored beard. "Shit, I've been planning on taking J. Claude's axe for a while. Right opportunity never came up until that crowd you attracted."

"Swoosh."

"I was in and out faster than you'd kiss a schoolboy."

"Glad I could be of service," Dynasty began playing a song that felt intimately familiar.

"You heard about what that idiot did in Missoula, right?"

"Picked a fight in real J. Claude style, from what I understand."

"No, man. That bastard broke my brother's jaw and kicked

my mama in the stomach." The dungeon of Rogers' gut gave loud signs of indigestion, he slugged more bourbon. "What kind of asshole does that?"

"Only one I can think of," Denny spoke solemnly, focusing on a song Rusty knew by heart. It was the tune J. Claude played every night as an encore and a tribute to his hometown.

Until then, the guitar hadn't taken a moment to consider what underhanded methods delivered him to that backroom. Rusty didn't like being stolen. He enjoyed Kenny and Dynasty talking nasty about his owner even less. Sure, it was fun to go out and be played by some new guys, but this negative attitude brought back a strong loyalty.

Denny sang in a soft tone:

I love you Memphis
You know I love you so
And I'd rather be here
Than any other place I know

It was Jimmie Rodgers' classic, Memphis Yodel, and Claude brought the house down with it each night, claiming it was a song about his favorite lady of all: Memphis, Tennessee. The gnawing pain of guilt was fully upon Rusty at that point.

"I'm not stopping with stealing this guitar," Kenny growled.

Dynasty, drunkenly missing a few chords, stopped. "Oh?"

"I picked this up at a police auction last year. They confiscated all of J. Claude's guns after he shot his publicist. Remember that crazy shit? Funny thing is, that publicist is still working for him. Must be givin' it to her nightly."

A long silver revolver made an appearance, slipping from a holster under Kenny's jacket.

"Anyway, I bought the entire lot. This one is supposedly Shakespeare's favorite."

"That's a biggie."

Kenny's eyes were lost in the chrome reflection. "I'll kill that bastard with his own gun next time I see him. Nobody should kick a grandma."

"Relax, big fella. Let uncle Denny take a look at that piece. Easy, easy now."

Kenny let the heavy artillery slip into Dynasty's soft hands. He looked at it for a few minutes and laid the gun across a case of mayonnaise.

Rogers' words were soaked wet and 150 proof: "That guitar and that gun are all I have left in life."

"Wow, talk about drama. What about your wife and grandkids? Your fans? Rotisserie chickens?"

"I'm telling you. That gun and guitar, that's all that matters. Might as well be dead without the burn they make in my belly. Stronger than this rotgut shit," he sipped whiskey from the bottle.

Denny swallowed a drunken hiccup. "I didn't know we were talking about dying and death fantasies. You're a deep dude, Kenny Rogers."

"Killing J. Claude isn't my death fantasy. Offing Shakespeare is just a hobby. If I ever get cancer or scurvy, you know, something fatal," Rogers' voice was forceful. "I've got a stable near Memphis, out in the sticks, and I'm just going to jump on my horse and ride through the woods. Go out with some dignity like those elephants who wander off to die alone."

"Elephants? Okay, maybe deep wasn't the right word."

"When an elephant knows they've come to the end, they split from their herd and wander into the brush to die. No fussing, no bullshit. Scientists don't know why they do it, but they do. Every one of 'em." He stopped and growled deep, "I know why. For dignity's sake. Dignity is all a man has in his life, Denny." Rogers gasped after a long whiskey drink. "It all comes down to dignity. Like what J. Claude took from my brother and mama."

"Not me, I have a lot more than dignity going on in my

life." Rusty felt Denny's delicate fingers rub a spot of dirt and grease off the fretboard. "Like that magical moment on stage tonight. That's why I got into this business."

"Not to mention, it felt good watching our man Caruthers bawling like a Girl Scout with a splinter," Rogers took another pull from the bottle and slurred Memphis Yodel's chorus. Diamond booze droplets sparkled across his beard.

"You and I, Ken, we have harmony. Your timing was perfect," Dynasty said with pixyish delight.

"Well, Denny, I've sung The Gambler about two-bazillion times. You get a feel for it after the first million." He passed Dynasty the bottle, which stopped the sequins-clad singer from scooting closer. They were the only two left in the storage room. Dawn peeked between the window security bars.

"Kenny and Denny, Denny and Kenny," Dynasty said with a playful whistle in his voice. "Sounds good together, doesn't it?"

"Not bad." Rogers' voice was sloppy, his wrinkled eyes were a squint. "I love you Memphis…"

"We could really have a duet on our hands, partner. Make that crap with you and Dolly Parton sound like nursery rhymes."

"Denny, that's something I'll have to run past my manager," Rogers stood and sat the whiskey on a case of ketchup. He looked at Dynasty's mascara-filled eyes and picked it back up with a generous swig. "I need to be going. See my wife. Love my wife, Denny."

"Kenny, would you like to see something else?" Denny leaned the guitar against the wall and stood. "See a surprise I have for you? One I've never shown anyone."

Kenny's eyes popped out a touch. He smiled politely and backed a step. "That's sweet, Den, but it's late. I'm just going to grab this guitar and—"

"No," Dynasty yipped and slapped Kenny Rogers' hand away. "There's something about me you don't know. Would never guess." His voice was drunk and confidential.

The pair stood and stared with half-sealed sleepy eyes. Rusty didn't desire either as an owner. The guitar was a dirty husband after a one-night-stand. He just wanted to get back to his mate and patch things up. He was sorry and filled with overwhelming guilt.

"I pinched that guitar fair and square," Rogers' voice was confused and hurt.

"Just let me borrow it for a few days," Dynasty placed his manicured hand on Kenny's rugged paw. "I have some plans for old Rusty."

Rogers snapped fingers back. "Just keep it. I'll get it later." He shook his head and left the room.

Minutes later, Denny Dynasty buried Rusty alive in that velvet-lined case.

"What does Denny want with me?" Rusty thought from the bowels of darkness. "I mean, I like Denny and all, but this is a funny way to show how much you care about a guitar. J. Claude never kept me in a case. This isn't dignity."

SIXTEEN

"Reading fan mail is the only thing better than sexing up a few dozen ladies after a show. It's the one thing that gives me the wholeness, you know? That oomph!"
    -J. Claude Caruthers, *Nashville's Shakespeare*

"Come on already, read me," the letter said. Fresh from having its envelope opened and being unfolded—it was ready to work. Its thick, expensive paper felt good in human hands again. Unfortunately, the little guy in a cowboy hat just held the crisp white letter to the light and stared. The others were quiet while this went on.

A moist mildew odor breathed off the rotting wood surrounding this group.

They stood circled on the porch, listening to the house shift and groan against the wind. A shutter hung by a single nail and slapped the side of the house.

"Well, what does it say?" asked the guy who looked exactly like the cowboy, except with about twenty extra pounds and a ponytail.

The letter had been waiting for half an hour. Ever since that pink scarf fella pulled it from the mailbox. But just as things were getting good, this chubby guy stumbled through the weeds. And, of course, there was a lot of yack-yack-yack about not seeing one another in thirty-five years, and boo-hoo-hoo I sure missed you brother, and huggidy-hug I'm so proud of you, let's try and be friends until the end.

"Meanwhile," the letter complained. "I'm here, full of useful info, and Dumbass holds me like a centerfold."

"It ain't nothing. Just a letter from the fire department requesting another donation," J. Claude said, bunching the letter in his fist.

The others looked quite stunned for a moment before Judy rescued the wad. "Let's double check, okay?"

The letter impatiently tapped its little paper foot waiting for this woman to finish, whispering its text under her breath. Meanwhile, the corners of its page flapped in the breeze, pissing the letter off fairly good.

"Well?" The womanish creature calling herself Denny, said. "What is it?"

"Lloyd, you might want to have a look."

The ponytail man laid a hand on the woman's shoulder. A jolt ripped through the letter. The paper huffed and puffed impatiently as it was passed. "Come on, come on, this is dynamite information. Read me. Now. I swear I'll give you a paper cut."

A zing of excitement rushed through the letter's fibers as this new man slid a finger across each line. "Mhhhhph," Lloyd's throat knowingly grumbled.

"Alright, I was just kidding about the firemen," J. Claude made an uncomfortable chuckle. "You know, my eyes were too tired to read over that letter. I haven't slept in sixteen days, brother. What…what did it, uh, you know, say?"

Lloyd's lips unhinged slightly and sighed, only to stall and play with his shirt cuff. "Well…" voice poured from his mouth with magma thickness.

Judy jumped over this grenade of silence, covering everything: "Time travel, something about your sister traveling through time and…and…" Judy's face bent in a way the letter had seen young children do when they drank milkshakes too fast.

"Ziggy?" J. Claude harnessed Judy's shoulders and shook until her focus centered on his severe facial lines.

The woman ran fingers through red hair. The letter liked being near Judy, her skin was stained with soft vanilla perfume. "Some business about helping escape the black hole."

"What a sister!" Denny Dynasty squealed with envy.

J. Claude stepped back until his shoulder blades were tight against paint speckled siding. His face was a maze of confused wrinkles. "I don't," Claude's mouth stumbled and wiggled. "I don't understand."

Another of Lloyd's long sighs watered down the dense confusion. "Relax," the physicist said.

"Lloyd?" Judy spoke. "How can you expect us to relax?"

He shrugged, "Zygmut's been talking about black holes for years."

SEVENTEEN

"I'll sleep when I'm six dirty-ass feet under."
  -J. Claude Caruthers, *Nashville's Shakespeare*

Humming Stella to calm his nerves, J. Claude Caruthers began tumbling toward sleep in the most unlikely of places.

With his head propped against a rusty faucet and those abbreviated legs curled inside his childhood bathtub, J. Claude collapsed—with a heavy amount of gravity—into dreams. Like most dreams, it began dark and disorienting, but soon the country legend was playing in the yard with this twin brother, it was the early sixties and life was a song. Lloyd and Claude wore coonskin caps and ducked around trees, firing invisible guns.

This was a pleasant surprise, since the majority of J. Claude's dreams since 1977 revolved around watching his wife's motorcycle land short of the ramp and burst into flames.

J. Claude thought this childhood vision was a sign. Maybe getting a little bit of his family back helped turn some corner. Perhaps now he could move beyond Stella's painful death.

Claude didn't spy on his childhood for very long, because two soft hands shook him awake. When J. Claude's eyes opened, Denny Dynasty stood over with a hungry look across that tight face. It was the same face J. Claude made when Jesus was late delivering a club sandwich. With the last of the day's light sneaking through the window, the singer couldn't tell the room was caked in layers of dirt and exposed wood. The toilet was split into three pieces. Some wild animal used a hole in the floor as a lavatory. Hazy tree shadows swayed across the walls.

"I thought you were Judy," Caruthers' voice was a bag of sawdust. "Those are some serious lady hands you got there, pal."

Dynasty stood tall with hands upon hips. "Wouldn't you like to know?"

"Take that show somewhere else, please. Get on out of here. This was the only place I found to get some shuteye and you douche it up." Nashville's Shakespeare lifted a threatening fist.

"You think you can take me? I'm not some redneck grandma from Montana. And I'm not her crippled son."

"Close it." His hands went into tight balls.

"Did you know those two were related to Kenny Rogers? You're a real scumbag."

"Did I know at the time? No." His fist dropped beneath the tub line. Claude leaned back and closed his eyes. "Those two were throwing bottles and calling me dickhead in the middle of a show. Get this, the son was the concert promoter. What would you have done, Denny? Shit, probably've given the guy a backrub and a tonguebath."

"Boy, you got me pegged. Tonguebaths and old men. Yum."

"They didn't look old and fragile when they were chucking glass at my head, I'll tell you that."

Dynasty shrugged without much interest. "No time to sleep, little buddy. There's work to be done." Denny rapidly tapped the tub with his foot, annoying Caruthers.

J. Claude lifted his exhausted body from its makeshift bed. His boot heels made a porcelain drum skin of the tub. Denny lent a hand, which J. Claude released like it was coated in spiders once his balance settled. Claude's eyeballs ached for relief. His mind was foggy and dense with sleepless confusion. "What's your deal? Why are you here, Dynasty?"

"If you think it's because I'm aiming to give you a tonguebath, keep dreaming. Hell, you still haven't written a song about me."

"What's the point? I had one more to go."

"Duh."

"But, I figure, who'd hear it? Even if the world wasn't ending, I'm starting to realize nobody'd care anyhow."

Denny folded his hands and let slim shoulders relax to the point of complete femininity. This pity made J. Claude uncomfortable.

"Out of my way, twinkletoes," Claude moved toward the door. "What work do we have that's so dang important?"

Denny led Claude through the darkness. "Follow me, it's meeting time."

"Meeting with who?"

"Don't be scared, it's not Kenny Rogers' mom."

Their feet kicked scraps of wood and drywall. Denny stopped and crouched low. This made J. Claude nervous.

"Well, lookit here."

"No thanks. Can we just get out of this place?"

"It's a rubber hand. This thing looks like it's been buried under all this shit forever. Stumpy's probably been looking for it."

"We called him Cubby, not Stumpy." Claude leaned close and inspected the disgusting prosthetic chunk. "Oddly, I was Chubby and he was Cubby. Guess time reversed us."

"You're not as svelte as you think, my man."

J. Claude swung a boot into Dynasty's leg. "C'mon, let's get out of here before we step on a nail or something."

Out the door and through the weeds, J. Claude discovered a comforting sight. Yellow beams from the bus windows met Memphis blackness with the knifing strength of a coastal lighthouse. Caruthers shuffled through the loose gravel at double normal pace. Denny wouldn't shut up about the fake hand.

Inside, everyone, including Jesus, sat around the bus' foldout dinner table. It looked like they were ready to play RISK, but there were no pieces on the board.

"Hell's going on in my bus?" Claude said. "You woke me up for this?"

"Have a seat, fellas," Lloyd said. He click-clacked a Zippo with nervous regularity. "I have a lot to tell everyone."

"So you've been gone for thirty years and now you're in charge, Lloyd?"

"I...oh...is that what it looks like?"

"Aw hell, maybe I'll go to some science lab and study astronauts."

"It's astrophysics. I study astrophysics—"

"Easy." Denny giggled and tossed a soiled rubber hand on the table with a wet smack. "We brought presents."

Lloyd gave it a curious look and quickly stowed it by his feet. "Thank you, but we have important matters to discuss."

"Hey, this is my bus. I think I should be calling the meetings to order around here. I don't even know what we're meeting about."

Lloyd's cheeks filled with blood. "Fine. Whatever gets us started. You have the floor."

J. Claude looked from face to face with disappearing purpose. "What's the point? We're all dead." Claude had been asking that question a lot and his recent nap was an opportunity to escape. Nashville's Shakespeare couldn't come up with an answer, so he let sleep smother him with hopes of black holes ending all these questions.

"That is the point," Lloyd said, adjusting thick glasses with smeared lenses. "Without the proper computer programs and statistical data, I'm not as confident as I'd like to be. God, I haven't done calculus on paper since high school. But, stick with me here, if my calculations are right, we don't have to die."

"Good god," Claude said, saddling up to the table. "What did Ziggy's letter say? I didn't look it over, it sounded pretty scientific. Too much for a hick like me."

"It wasn't the letter, it's something I thought of earlier."

"Will someone tell me what all this bullshit about time traveling is?" Jesus' left eye was growing huge and veiny, a look J. Claude only saw when the bacon supply was low.

"Relax, take it easy. The bullshit is just that, bullshit," Lloyd calmly said. "I'd been receiving letters like this for decades. I assumed it was some prank. It stopped recently, so I guessed the joker was bored or dead." The scientist winced an apology to his brother. "Regardless, time travel is impossible."

"Wait, how do you know that?" Dynasty said. "I mean, isn't the world getting eaten by some magical black nothing? What does impossible have to do with anything? This shit's enough to make me start keeping my eyes peeled for the tooth fairy."

"It's not magic. It's physics. Trust me, it's a long story. Okay, how about this? Aside from the physical impossibility, if time travel existed, wouldn't we know it? Wouldn't people from the future be here bragging? It's human nature. We're the worst secret keepers I know. It's like I always say, when science closes a door, nature busts in a hundred windows. Think about the complications a discovery like time travel would create."

"Wait, wait, boogie the truck on back here," sweat beaded into a crown around J. Claude's hairline. "You've been awfully quiet about this talking to our sister business. Why didn't you tell me?"

"Chubby, I just assumed she was in touch with you, too. And, the letters weren't much, the contact was always one-way. Her rattling on about physics equations or sharing a cab with Barak Obama's great grandchild. A lot of time travel bologna, like this letter."

"Why didn't you tell me?" Claude's voice was loud, his hands knotted into fists.

"You and I weren't exactly speaking. Honestly, I always got the impression you two spent time together and I was the odd man out. Those letters made it sound like you were both in Nashville."

"So, wait," Judy held up a hand. "She was telling you about traveling through time?" Her shoulder was a flinch away from Lloyd's. Asking the question, she leaned in so they touched.

"Oh, now, come on. Be reasonable. Time travel is something H.G. Wells made up. Don't read too much into what I said."

"No idiot, Michael J. Fox invented time travel. Little something called *Back to the Future*." J. Claude stood, started humming Stella a little until his leg stopped shaking. "Okay, this conversation ain't over. But let's hear about this plan, mister astrophysicist."

"Asshole physicist is more like it," Denny said under his breath. "I want that fake hand back. I could use it for things."

"Hey, that's my brother." J. Claude shouted.

"Not necessary, fellas," Lloyd's scientific monotone cut Denny's next zinger off. "Now, what I'm going to tell you is difficult to understand, but, basically, I'm talking about a white hole."

Denny giggled and started to speak with a smirk.

"Cram it," J. Claude landed a sharp elbow into Denny's side. "I'm looking for an excuse to kill you, Dynasty. Damn that twenty-four hour gun license." He fired a look to his publicist.

"So, like I was saying," Lloyd commanded attention. "A black hole works like this." He lifted the RISK board so the entire globe was flat. He placed the flaming lighter under Europe and let the orange glow eat through the board until a crumbling hole rolled from Switzerland north, south, east and west. Flames and grey ashy flecks swirled to the ceiling until Lloyd blew out the blaze leaving nothing but campfire smell.

The group saw a massive hole just barely touching the Eastern Seaboard of the United States.

"I have no idea where this thing is, but it's moving slower than anticipated. There's a theory to fix the problem I created."

"You created?" almost everyone at the table said.

"Hold on just a minute," Claude said.

"Lloyd?" Judy was hushed and spoke through a tight jaw.

"Oh, of course," Dynasty chirped. "This is perfect."

"I'll explain later, I promise." He held his lone hand. Lloyd Caruthers was in charge. "But for now you all have to promise me something."

Judy's face grew sour. "You're asking us to keep a secret? I thought we were the worst at secrets." She bit her lip and slid a length of red bangs behind her ear like a woman on a date.

"That's perfect, because I want you to do the exact opposite, actually," Lloyd's voice was jovial, but his face was stiff as a plank.

The group reluctantly agreed.

"If I fix our problems, if I can put a stop to the end of the world, you have to spread the news that I am responsible. I deduced a way to save the planet. You have to help my name live on forever."

EIGHTEEN

"Shit happens. Sometimes that's just the way the crumble cookies, you know?"

-J. Claude Caruthers, *Nashville's Shakespeare*

"Wow, Denny," Lloyd yelled over the motor's shaking clatter. He slammed the hood and muffled the mechanical knocks. Moonlight bounced off the car's white shell as the smell of combustion found his nostrils. "When you're right, you're right. All I had to do was touch those two wires and the engine started right up."

"Something every red-blooded man should know."

"Then how'd you learn it?"

"Oh, Mister Black Hole has a sense of humor," Denny was over the top with fluttering eyelashes and curved lips. "Let's just say you learn a lot in my line of work."

Dynasty jumped in the driver's seat.

Lloyd settled into the passenger side and made a face. "You need to hotwire a lot of cars as a gay country singer?"

Denny put the stolen Buick into gear and began driving back toward the Caruthers homestead. "That's not quite what I meant, but oh well, that's the way the crumble cookies, right?"

They shared a laugh.

"Having an extra set of wheels is nice, but I must disagree. I don't see how it helps my plan. I have a lot of thinking to do about this white hole business," Lloyd said. "Back in Switzerland, we needed seventeen miles of space and a particle accelerator for a remote shot at creating a Big Bang. And now we're talking about a theory even rarer than collapsing stars. I doubt I'll be so lucky."

"Lucky?" Denny hissed. "Poor choice of words, brother."

"That's not quite what I meant, but as a wise man once told me, 'that's the way the crumble cookies.'"

"You think that's my line, don't you?"

"It's not?"

"No," Denny paused, trying to sense if he was being put on. "I stole it from your brother's book."

"Really? I never read it."

"You never read your own brother's biography?" Denny eyed the astrophysicist for a long while, deciding how to take this. "I like you more and more, you know?"

Lloyd was surprised and pleased they shared a second laugh.

Lit trees flashed through the windshield space. For the singer and scientist, all was blackness outside the womb of headlights. A long quiet built between them for nearly a minute.

"Lloyd, you don't have to feel so guilty," Denny said, squinting into the darkness as he steered.

"Guilty," his words deflated slowly. "About the book?"

"No, stupid."

"What, exactly, would I feel guilty about?"

"I used to study physics, too," Dynasty said. "I really loved reading about Bob Oppenheimer."

"Same here."

"Know what the J stands for in J. Robert?"

"Easy one, nothing. Just like Claude, the J is just a J."

"Very good."

"I'm a huge admirer of his work. I foll—"

"The J is just a J. Research is just research, you know? What was it Opp said toward the end of his life? About inventing something that killed thousands and could someday lead to the destruction of the entire planet?"

Lloyd sounded stiff, "I don't recall."

Denny's voice boomed loud. Not the bird melody pipes he used on stage, but something as solid and powerful as a movie trailer announcer. "'Scientists are not delinquents. Our work has changed the conditions in which men live, but the use made of these changes is the problem of governments, not of scientists.'"

"I think I have heard that."

"He's saying it's not a scientist's fault when shit enters fan. If people had to first worry about consequences, we'd never have built planes because one day they might fly into skyscrapers and kill people. Think of all the laser-guided missile technology that stems from NASA missions. The men who put astronauts on the moon don't lose sleep over their relationship to dead babies in Baghdad. What I'm saying is you can't let this guilt, guilt you're clearly holding, get under your skin."

Lloyd nodded. The man had a point. The physicist needed to scrap any old sentiments if his work was to live.

Lloyd badly wanted this talk to end, though. It made him sweaty and stung his nub.

"Denny, thank you for this hand." He raised his arm. "It's from when I was in high school. It was my first prosthetic. It's a little small now, but it cleans up nice, don't you think?" He held rubberized flesh between them.

"You never forget your first time," he cracked. "It's a classic, Lloyd. Totally matches your eyes."

They didn't speak the next few miles as the stolen car groped down more black, tree-lined Tennessee roads.

Just before the headlights spread across the Cape Cod's driveway, Denny spoke. "Were you serious about that immortality stuff?"

Lloyd's throat cleared. His good hand squeezed the rubber one flat. "I have a lot of faith in my work. I've spent my entire life with physics. I'm not going to give up when physics needs me most." That throat made another racket, "whenever science closes a door—"

"Right, right, right, windows and whatnot, gotcha. But what does being a hero have to do with physics?"

"Well," Lloyd's face grew red and a sweaty glaze formed on his back. "I'm just interested in making sure doomsday idiots don't, you know, credit things to a miracle or whatnot."

"Wouldn't it be a miracle if you saved the world?"

"You know those two don't coexist in physics. Miracles and science."

The singer rolled his eyes. "I spotted you from a mile away, Lloyd Caruthers," Denny was now sounding slippery. "You can't fool me. Little brother's had all the attention and you see your chance to climb past him on the ladder."

"No," disgusted venom spewed from Lloyd's lips.

"Brother, you're talking to a man who set his gunsight on immortality years ago. Don't be shy. Everyone wants to live forever. Why do you think some son of a bitch climbed Mount Everest? Because it was there? Bullshit, nobody wants to think they'll be forgotten when their skull is a pile of dust. That's why people started keeping history books. Hell, the history book inventor probably figured he'd get in the damn things for being the first to create history."

"Mhhhhhph," Lloyd grunted, pawing this idea over in his mind, thinking it passed the scientific reasoning test. Lloyd wondered if his heroes ever wasted time thinking about immortality and getting credit. He wondered if they ever lost a girl like Veronique. Ever had a pain-in-the-ass brother. Was there a J. Claude Einstein he'd never heard of?

Dynasty spoke: "It's probably natural, though. Same reason most people have some urge to make babies." Lloyd blushed at his recent wish for family. "Why did cavemen paint on walls? Because everybody knows their time is limited, but nobody wants to think they wasted it. But the truth probably is, there's nothing you can do to make it worth your while."

"Denny, do you always talk like this?"

"Not usually. I'm normally talking about hair spray and re-cording contracts. But maybe it's knowing that black beastie is out there. Maybe it's having a genius in the passenger seat. Something's got ahold of me. We have to stop this thing."

"I agree." Lloyd's face made a painful squeeze. He slipped fingers around the rubber wrist and massaged the stump.

"Like I was saying, that's why nobody says this stuff out loud. It's buried deep in the back of the brain, right next to where a man like you hides his," Denny whispered the next lines, "homosexual urges."

The car jumped to a stop, skittering a little in the gravel.

"Oh wow, we're already home. Look at that," Lloyd's voice was stiff and scientific. He unbuckled and crawled from the car.

Denny followed suit. "Okay, Mister Brains, you go into the bus and wrap your head around this one. I'm going to go snoop through this place. I always loved spooky secret places as a kid. You know, if I'm going to bite it, might as well go out reliving happy childhood memories."

"Sounds like a plan," Lloyd said, not even turning to ac-knowledge Dynasty.

Safely inside the bus, the physicist released a tense breath he'd swallowed back in the car. He let all that weirdness dis-appear. There was a strange connection to Denny Dynasty, but not in the sort of man-on-man connection the Queen of Nashville probably imagined. There was a comfortable famil-iarity, like Lloyd could predict what Denny was going to say.

"Did you guys steal a car?" J. Claude said, raiding the kitch-en cupboards, tossing out bags of marshmallows and loaves of rye bread.

"Denny thinks it'll come in handy."

"What, are you going to race a black hole?" He ripped a drawer forward and clattered through utensils.

"Hopefully it won't come to that. I need to do some serious thinking." Lloyd watched a long silver butcher knife send beams of light around the bus while his brother removed it. "Cooking?"

"No, just for security. You know, in case there are looters roaming the woods or something."

"Brilliant." Lloyd popped off the rubber hand with a suction cup squish. His stump was moist with sweat. "The end of the world is here and I'm sure people are stealing jewelry."

"You just stole a car."

"Forget it. Box yourself up. I'm sure it'll all turn out fine."

"You know, Lloyd, you don't have to act like I'm some sort of retarded baby."

"Excuse me?" Claude's snap was a surprise. Lloyd wasn't excited about arguing with men carrying sharp objects.

"I forgot what a freaking drag you were to be around. I never felt like such a piece a shit my whole life as when I was near you." He tucked the blade in his jeans. "Thirty years hasn't changed much—"

"You blew off my hand," Lloyd momentarily forgot about the knife.

"It was an accident. Besides, what the hell were you playing scientist for? We should have been out looking for mom and dad and Ziggy." Claude edged closer with the threat of menace from that knife. "You know a reporter once asked me why we were doing all that after they disappeared and I realized I didn't know."

"Science," his eyes closed, trying to clear the harsh tone from his voice. "Has always helped me deal with stress and see things clearly. Probably like when you write a song. Except you probably never lost a limb songwriting."

"It was an accident. Jeez," he screamed.

Tension and poison ripped from Lloyd's throat: "You're illiterate, Claude. I asked you to pour beaker B into beaker F. God knows what you did, but I think we all see the results." Lloyd held up his stump and the phantom pain returned like car doors crushing flesh, crushing bone.

"See, you always make me feel stupid. So what if I can't read? I sure as hell can count and I've made about two bazillion dollars. Wrote a couple thousand songs. Millions of people are happy because of me. Forget reading, has reading physics ever made anyone happy? Sounds to me like it just makes people miserable or dead."

Lloyd grasped his ponytail and slid a fist down it. "That's not fair."

"Nobody ever died from a country song."

"Weren't you playing a country song when Stella jumped those buses?" Guilt instantly knocked Lloyd with heavyweight force to the stomach.

"Well, now it's official," J. Claude removed the knife and pointed it at his brother, though they were too far away to touch. "I liked you better when we were estranged."

J. Claude stomped to the back of the bus and slammed the door.

In the minutes of silence that followed, Lloyd brewed a pot of coffee and stared at an empty pad of paper. Clicking coffee percolations held his focus, instead of scribbling equations. He was counting how many hollow pops came from the machine during a ten second span. Then he multiplied it so he could know how many burbles were in an hour, a day and the month of March.

Lloyd had no idea where to begin this white hole business. A white hole, after all, was just a theory. Though black holes were considered a theory by hard line scientists before yesterday.

Inadvertently creating a black hole took over a decade of research and preparation. Giving birth to its polar opposite on a tight time budget caused the phantom hand to vibrate with agonizing cathedral bells.

Three mugs of coffee had washed down Lloyd's throat and the pad of paper was still empty when Denny returned to the bus. "Check this out." His face was sunken but with a glimmer of amazement.

The scientist's elbows were on the table, his stump and hand cradled his face. "Huh?" Lloyd said, mind swallowed by a dark pit of thought.

Denny laid down a dusty book. It was warped with water damage and its faded leather cover said, "Diary."

"Probably my sister's," Lloyd said with no enthusiasm for nostalgia.

"I think you're right. Check this shit out."

Lloyd leafed through the thick, crusty pages. Their formation fit together like spoons in a drawer. The ink was hazy.

"Nice, thanks." He slid it away.

"You missed it," Denny said. "Look at this."

Dynasty flipped the book open until one faded page stared Lloyd in the face. The handwriting was familiar. The physicist's neck craned over the book and he read aloud. Each word took on a bigger tone of disbelief than the previous. "White Hole Recipe, by Zygmut Caruthers."

NINETEEN

"Some sons-a-guns just don't know when to quit. Not me, hoss. I'll know when my time under the bright light is up."
   -J. Claude Caruthers, *Nashville's Shakespeare*

The knife was lonesome. Its stainless steel body shuddered cold in the bus' darkness, even with seductive moonlight glowing across her silver parts. That by itself should have felt like something ghostly and magical. But this knife, she was never satisfied.

"I miss Jesus," she pouted. "I miss dicing and chopping and jullienneing." She used to get a thrill every time the chef slid four toothpicks into a club sandwich and sliced up quarters. Through the toast, the lettuce, the tomato, the bacon, more toast, the ham, the turkey and more toast, it was a pure, powerful task.

It'd been forever since she gave a sandwich the business. She felt dull and unimportant. The knife had heard muffled voices through the drawer. Apparently the entire planet was dying. Little pops of anxiety filled the blade, made her want to slice and dice and chop and mince until that moment came. She was comfortable with dying quickly. She never liked the idea of growing outdated and rusty in some thrift store.

"Speaking of growing outdated," she chuckled as J. Claude Caruthers paced the darkness. He'd rescued the knife from its drawer an hour or two ago. He muttered about being tired and not getting any shuteye. He mentioned how Lloyd's coffee smelled good, but he'd be damned if he crawled back to that asshole for a cup. Claude once fell onto the bed and the knife heard the singer's breathing regulate like sleep, but car doors slammed and an automobile pulled away, snapping gravel beneath its tires.

"Who the hell is leaving at this hour?" the knife wondered.

Since then, Caruthers sat in the high stool against the window, holding the knife in his callused hands, rubbing the hard fingertips together. "You're dead, Claude," he spoke with his head against the glass, fogging it with each breath. "No amount of pushing and fighting will fix it."

The singer discharged a long, slow breath that seemed to have decades of sadness and motivation tangled within it. The knife recognized the man shared her sentiments on dying. Better to go out in a quick flicker than become useless.

"I'll see you real soon, Stella. I can't wait, honestly. Dying sounds nice, knowing we'll be together. I don't know why I was waiting to finish Zygmut before doing this," he rubbed his eyes with a free hand. "So tired," his voice was a few heartbeats shy of belonging in a morgue.

J. Claude turned his wrist toward heaven and, with the silver point of the knife, read his veins like Braille. Each blood vessel rose above the skin—a hump of dirt covering a fresh grave. The sharp blade tensed as they touched. This was not the kind of job she was hoping for.

"It's no club sandwich, but still," her opinion shifted. "Work feels good."

After a few minutes of nearly opening his wrist, Claude tossed the knife on the bed, veins intact.

Without warning, a slow, sad melody cut through the silence and scared the blade. Claude was singing with his lips closed.

"Good timing, Claude," he spoke, mocking.

Caruthers sat drumming a finger against the window,

watching the moon feed between tree gaps. It left a ghostly coat of primer over the crooner's childhood home. He repeatedly hummed a pattern and his lips gently smacked together, muttering.

"Zygmut," a growl of discomfort emerged from his golden throat, "somehow I knew you'd come when I didn't need you anymore," he told the empty room. "Guess I should've gotten serious about suicide a few years back. Maybe I could have finished it then." He chuckled and cleared his throat as the words to his elusive song formed.

Like a moonbeam
or a star
Like the Queen of England
and King Tut
You didn't seem real, my Ziggy
My long, lost Zygmut

Claude paused and silently mouthed the words again. He made a few false starts before repeating the brief collection of lines.

The knife laughed, "Wow, that's terrible."

J. Claude also laughed. "Wow, that's terrible." A stiff smile broke under his mustache and, with the moonlight working its magic, his teeth glowed a black light's sheen. "But it's a start."

The singer began digging through his midnight dark closet. The shadows of shirts and hats landed on the bed next to the blade. "Where the hell is that tape recorder?" He crawled from the closet. "I can't lose this song, even if it's trash."

For several decades Claude recorded every song idea onto a tape recorder. The tapes were actually converted into a mildly successful rarities box set five years earlier.

Humming the melody, he opened his door and walked through the bus. Nashville's Shakespeare was overcome with an urge to find that little microcassette recorder.

A sight in the moon haze ended his search. A dense stiffness set his back rigidly straight.

Expecting to see his brother hard at work, Claude stopped searching for the microcassette, realizing the room was dark and empty. But something in the shadows bent his mood. J. Claude nearly began snarling. A dense trickle of slobber cupped to the corner of his mouth.

Claude rushed back to the room and grabbed the knife.

"Just catching a few winks, huh, Denny?" The singer mumbled, gripping the knife with choking intensity. "My life was great before you came on the scene. And since that day, you've tried everything to ruin me. Now," Claude said a hint louder, "I've had enough."

A moment later, the knife saw more action than she ever imagined. The bus was empty except for Denny Dynasty sleeping on the fold-out couch. She was disoriented when J. Claude's voice boomed through the silence.

"Up and at 'em, princess."

The knife felt Denny Dynasty's throat tense as its sharp side rested against a meaty jugular.

"Claude?" he stuttered.

"Looks like you and me are the only ones here. Looks like I've had enough of your shit. If I'm going to die, I've decided I don't want Denny Dynasty anywhere near me when it happens."

"Claude, calm down," a tone of feminine worry filtered through Denny's throat.

"You're always making fun of me, copying me," the knife crept into the flesh. The blade felt showered in purpose. Suddenly, she knew why people worked at nuclear waste dumps and scrubbed toilets for a living. They weren't the most glamorous lines of work, but finishing a job felt good. She understood, at that moment, J. Claude's need to finish one last song. She was not a violent knife, but was suddenly caught in the action and looked forward to opening Denny's throat.

"It's not what you think," Dynasty's voice fell to a raspy skitter.

"Goodbye, Denny. I should have done this years ago."

The knife felt itself lifting off the neck for momentum. J. Claude's hand was shaky, but seemed focused on finishing this grizzly job.

Both men's lungs froze. The knife tensed with anticipation. There was a blue flash when the trees stopped blowing in the breeze, stopped stenciling moonlit shadows. For a second, J. Claude's eyes were the only thing moving, clearly asking himself for assurance, because things were getting close to the point of no return.

Some little storm cloud in his skull reported back with an affirmative. His eyes said sliding this knife across Denny's throat was just the prescription. And besides, if everyone was going to die, what was the harm?

Claude's muscles twitched toward the neck and Denny made a final gasp. "I'm Zygmut."

Claude stopped his arm and little flecks of enamel chipped from his grinding teeth.

Denny's frame was tense, his lips hardly parted, his voice was cigarette scarred. "It's me. I'm your big sister."

"Bullshit." Claude lifted the blade higher this time. The knife was ready to plunge down this rollercoaster hill.

"I came back to help you and Lloyd. I knew this black hole was going to happen. I'm from the future. We all know about Lloyd then. Mom and Dad sent me to make sure it actually happens."

"Oh, like *Terminator*, huh?"

"Claude, you have to listen."

"No, this is all pretty convenient. You just saw that letter from Ziggy and this knife and another golden opportunity to screw with J. Claude popped into your brain, didn't it, Dynasty?"

The wilting growl continued: "I wrote that letter. I figured you two would catch on." Denny's lungs desperately pumped for oxygen. His body dug backward, deeper into the mattress' squeaky security.

"Nice try. Enjoy singing about gay angels up there in heaven," he took the knife down to the soft skin above Denny's clavicle, but paused. Claude swallowed hard.

"What in the hell is going on?" the knife was thoroughly freaked.

"I can tell you your biggest secret," Dynasty's mouth stole enormous, frightened breaths. "Something you didn't mention in your biography. Something you never even told Stella."

Claude's lips were stiff. His eyes jumped out of the darkness with the sparkly look of a warrior. "I'll give you until the count of three."

Denny cleared his throat with a strain, careful not to push closer into the blade.

"One…" The knife glittered full of moonlight. "Two…"

"You're not illiterate." Dynasty released a thin huff. "You used to read Hardy Boys mysteries to me before mom and dad tucked you in."

Time began winding forward again, those black trees swayed and juggled blue light into the bus.

The knife slipped from Claude's hand and clattered to the floor. She was woozy with the drama and didn't even feel her sharp point dull against the linoleum.

With eyes bursting large, J. Claude latched Dynasty's shoulders. "Who told you that lie?"

Denny, or who Claude thought was Denny, made a confident wink. "You know how I know."

"What is going on here…" He stuttered and cleared his throat. "Z-Ziggy?" he said, unsure.

Dynasty sat up and latched a hand over his throat. His voice was dark and full of scratches. "I'll explain everything. But for now, help me get into the luggage compartment."

"You got some futuristic super weapon we need to save the planet? Is it a white hole machine?"

Dynasty made a face that asked Claude: what are you smoking? "No, Claude, I have Rusty. That son-of-a-bitch Kenny Rogers stole it. But I beat the shit out of him and took it back for you."

"Why?"

"You're going to need Rusty."

TWENTY

"My daddy always told me, 'Cryin' ain't gonna get you anything but wet.'"

-J. Claude Caruthers, *Nashville's Shakespeare*

The stolen car was confused. Lloyd gripped the steering wheel the way he wrung water from sponges. Jesus punched at the radio buttons until tiny bruised dots formed on his fingertips. From the back, Judy kicked the passenger seat while she snapped the diary's pages over and over. The car wanted to know why it deserved such abuse.

Memphis before dawn was surprisingly bustling. The car called out for help, but none of the other automobiles listened. He was hijacked, but it didn't seem to matter. The traffic grew thick while dull streaks of daybreak appeared over stoplights in the swinging summer wind. Every church the car passed—from the newest stadium-seating models, to the crumbling brick steeples—was packed.

"Radio says there's no robbery, no riots, no panic anywhere," Jesus said with another twist of the dial, trying to find more news.

"Yeah, I got it. God, it's like I'm talking to Claude. We all heard the same report, you know," Lloyd said and winced, like these harsh words built another layer of ache in his belly. Since insulting his brother, the dry sting of stress seemed to constantly terrorize the physicist, setting off landmines and firing rounds of ammunition into his sensitive soul. Even the car could tell Lloyd's ability to pile on misery knew no limits.

Jesus changed the channel again and the car felt a tension from the new station. A golden voice with lush Nashville strings filled the speakers. The three bodies in the car stopped moving, even blinking.

Well I've tangoed in ballrooms
And sipped fine champagne

Lloyd dropped his gaze and wrapped his free arm around his chest.

And I've slept in the ditches
I've huffed gasoline

Jesus held a finger just over the radio button. He could have advanced the station at any moment, but didn't. His eyes closed, the car sensed his heart rate rise.

There weren't nothing in my life
To fill that lonely ravine
Until I made you my wife
Lovely, sweet Jeanine

Judy stopped gazing at that diary. She fed a strand of red hair into her mouth and began chewing.

Everyone was fixated and a timely sadness felt thick in the cabin. No one spoke until Jesus flipped the channel, causing each to release a buoyant breath "I'm sorry," he uttered with the next station's news of spreading doom.

"Thank you for doing that," Judy said, equally hushed.

"Do you hear this?" the chef said with a higher, urgent timbre. "I just can't believe people are giving up, dying."

"What else can we ask?" the scientist replied.

Jesus chuckled, fully lifting from that radio trance, from

that guilt of talking about J. Claude behind his back. "I was hoping you'd know, Doc." Previously, the entire carload was razzing the singer. "Why else are we collecting all this shit? Iffy time for a scavenger hunt."

"I didn't make us pick up Iberico Ham, I didn't make us grab seventeen-dollar-a-pound cheese, I didn't steal organic turkey breast from that shop. My stops were for science, Jesus. I doubt you can claim the same." The car was surprised by the condescending tone and noticed the physicist tense in the driver's seat, once again feeling rotten.

"That is the finest ham in the world. Those pigs've been raised from the same bloodline for centuries. That cheese is so good it'll make your pants tighter, you know what I'm saying? Man, if I can track down some high quality bacon we'll be set."

"Listen," Lloyd took a breath and gave a friendly pat to his shoulder. "Time is really at a premium, I just don't see how this factors into us stopping the problem at hand."

"Forget a white hole, we're all dead, man." Jesus' voice was amused. "Me, I'm making one dynamite club sandwich before we all go out."

"A sandwich? Now? I don't—"

"This place looks good," Judy said, leaning against the rear window for a view. "Jim Neely's Interstate Barbecue." A long brick building with a happy pink pig mural on the side came into focus. Like most of Memphis' barbecue hot spots, the paint was peeling, the handwritten notes in the window were sun-faded and it hadn't been redecorated since J. Claude's bus was still coated in showroom wax.

The main reason the car was confused came courtesy of the group's odd shopping list. Jesus' items seemed sensible compared to Lloyd and Judy's collection. By that point the scientist and the publicist rounded up a few hundred feet of copper wire, six car batteries, a stick of dynamite, two notebook computers and a bunch of electronic trash from a department store.

"What does a smoker even look like?" Judy said.

"It said we need one with at least one-hundred cubic feet of space, right?" Lloyd recalled.

"That's it, up here," Jesus stopped using his fingers to torture the radio dial and pointed. "My first job as a cook was at a barbecue joint like this way before I met Claude."

"The good old days," Judy muttered.

"Hey, watch it, babe. That dude's my best friend. J. Claude saved my ass."

"Get serious. Best friends?" she sounded puzzled. "I've never seen you two have more than a minute-long conversation and even then it's usually about whether mustard belongs on a club."

The chef spun around and eyed J. Claude's publicist. He looked as if something wild and dangerous was secretly dying his blood darker until it was black. "You don't get it, do you?"

The smoker was behind the restaurant. It was a retired propane tank—a capsule shaped like an enormous rusted aspirin. Smokestack pipes ran from its lid and the body was attached to a set of lawnmower tires. Unfortunately, the smoker was surrounded by a barbwire fence. Memphis had a crime rate almost mean enough to steal light back out of a black hole, but not quite. So even half-ton barbecue smokers were highly guarded.

Lloyd looked back at Judy, "What's wrong? Why are you making that face?"

The car could tell she was in pain, rubbing her shoulder. "I think it's going to storm."

"What?"

"My shoulder, it hurts whenever it's going to rain or when the weather changes abruptly. Arthritis courtesy of your brother."

"How did J. Claude give you arthritis?"

"Oh, probably the time he shot me. I'm still walking around with bullet fragments. When the sky turns, this thing claws to get out." Her fingers rubbed a long rosy scar a few shades lighter than her tangled hair.

Lloyd and Judy had eyes locked. His voice was soft and surprised: "That's kind of like my hand." He slipped off the old rubber mold and exposed the nub. "This thing always hurts like I still have fingers. It's all J. Claude's fault."

"Well," Judy had a vibrant look, though her throat sounded dry: "You and I are two peas." She grinned as Lloyd casually fixed his hair, almost like he didn't want her to see.

"Yeah," the car could tell that voice. Lloyd was seeing Judy differently. It sensed a nervous temperature rise in the cabin. The car had been a silent party on many first dates and back-seat romances and knew this scene well.

"What time do you think it is in New York?" Judy hid blushing cheeks.

"I'm thinking we need to ram the fence," Jesus said.

Lloyd didn't know who to answer first, so his lips stayed intimately close. The car knew his eyes never lifted from the woman in the back seat.

However, the car disagreed with Jesus' plan and promptly stalled. It held out as long as possible, hoping a police cruiser would pass and end this mess.

"I think I'm going to call my father," Judy said. "I bet he's awake now."

"Nothing wrong with that," Lloyd said, watching through the rearview mirror as she searched a black purse.

"Yeah. We haven't chatted in a while," she said with a smile that dominated her face. Judy hopped out of the car, holding a palm over one ear and the ringing phone to the other.

Also outside the car, Lloyd pulled in a fresh breath of dewy morning air while he popped the hood and touched those two hotwires again. Back behind the driver's seat, he and Jesus studied Zygmut's pencil-scratched diary on the arm rest.

"Last item on the list," Jesus said.

"Can I tell you something?"

"I guess. Nothing too mushy, though." He gave a queasy glance to Judy, standing outside the car.

"No, nothing like that." Lloyd sighed and let the engine run. White mist left the tailpipe and hovered over the bumper.

This made the car nervous. It liked its nose and wasn't in the mood for rhinoplasty. Every second trickled like water torture. He was a religious car and had faith in a bountiful afterlife where his oil was changed every three-thousand miles and he was cleaned and detailed a few times a year, but he wanted his time on Earth to be painless as possible.

"Stuff like this got us into this mess," Lloyd's palm made a papery smack on the diary. "If it wasn't for Zygmut's advice, I really doubt we'd be having this situation."

The chef stared ahead, as if nothing was said, slowly closing his eyes. "Man, talking like that doesn't do any good. This world's always moving forward. It's always busting chops. If it wasn't a black hole, it'd be some other garbage."

"No, I don't think you follow. I told you guys she'd been contacting me. Well, Zygmut wasn't just sending birthday cards and newspaper articles about our brother."

Jesus kept his face forward, his eyes crept open, looking beyond the windshield glare and over the high chain link fence with bright orange morning creeping above. The chef rubbed his face and the car caught a whiff of body odor—Jesus hadn't showered since learning about the damning radio reports.

"Everything Zygmut said was so good, so correct. Her notes helped me so much in Switzerland. Her equations earned me a position as the head physicist on my team. Good god, the last note she sent even explained how to give someone food poisoning, botulism."

"You lost me a long time ago."

"I'm just saying, she never mentioned the possibility of black holes. But look where we are? How am I supposed to know this diary will make things better? What if it's another, I don't know, another detour?"

The musky salt odor of sweat filled the car's cabin. "I don't know exactly what is going on, but this is what I tell my kids and wife." Jesus' nervous fingers gripped the seatbelt restraint. "Once in a while not screwing shit up is worse than trying to do something good and still messing everything to hell. We're going to die when this black hole finds Memphis, right?"

"Theoretically, yes. No one knows for sure what happens once a human crosses the Event Horizon—"

"Hell, let's go down taking a swing." He smacked the dashboard like an egg at breakfast. "The oyster is our world, right?" Jesus lifted a sleeve and revealed a tattoo.

"Hey, that's pretty catchy." He gave a polite smile. "Did you come up with that?"

"No…that's from…never mind."

Lloyd checked in the rearview and watched Judy's skirt flapping around her knees. His stare held for another moment before he shifted the car into gear and pounded down the fence in three tries.

The impact was the equivalent of fingernails and blackboards to the car. Its milky white hood, now scratched, mimicked the wandering lines of a topographical map. Its engine was fine, but battering ram duty annoyed the hell out of it.

The car really lost its temper when Lloyd didn't even take a minute to inspect the damage, he just walked over to that woman, his head shaking, his hand and nub jammed into pockets.

"Jesus is tying the smoker to the bumper, you ready to, ah," he said, reedy and sliced with nerves. "You know, ready to go?"

Her back was to Lloyd, the breeze still blowing her hem and exposing the back divots of knees. She turned to reveal a wet, pink face squinting with tears. Her mouth opened slowly, a fat scream couldn't quite crawl out.

"Judy," Lloyd said.

"I couldn't reach him," her words were soaked in mucus. "Daddy's phone was dead."

A pale, frightened look overcame the scientist. "Maybe there is a logical explanation…every problem has a reasonable solution if we just…" his voice disappeared. The wrinkles of dread deepened.

The car realized there was only one explanation. The dense crush of fatality was like he'd seen at a junkyard, those cars being mashed into metal cubes.

"I'm sorry," Lloyd clutched his stump and rubbed it.

Judy strained to say something more, but simply fell into Lloyd's arms. He squeezed as her knees melted. Jesus' metal clanking, attaching the rickety smoker to the bumper, filled the car with pain.

It couldn't tell, but judging by the spasms his back made, the tense jerking of his head, the car realized Lloyd was crying too.

The pair held one another as traffic buzzed past. Even though the roads were jammed with panicked drivers, no horns blew. The gentle sound of tires speeding across pavement was proof people were being polite, not wanting to hurt anyone's feelings, on their best behavior before dying. Had the people of Memphis moved on to the next step of the grieving process? Acceptance?

"We're ready to roll, guys," Jesus called, giving the chain a firm tug.

"Come on, we can save a lot of lives if this works. I think your father would like that." As Lloyd gently groaned, the car recognized the look of guilt wrapping fingers around Caruthers' throat.

Lloyd ushered Judy back to her seat with a warm arm around her shoulder.

TWENTY-ONE

"Every time I step on stage, I still get that Fourth-of-July-in-the-guts feeling I did of my first sold-out show."
  -J. Claude Caruthers, *Nashville's Shakespeare*

"J. Claude Caruthers," Denny Dynasty's voice was a blast of lightning. "Wake up. For god's sake, there's so much to do."

Since Dynasty's claim to the family bloodline, Nashville's Shakespeare sensed that phone call raspiness, but not much else different in his rival. "I can't help it. I haven't slept in weeks. My body is on...on...I don't know, what's worse than autopilot?"

"Do you want to stay alive?" the possible sister said, eyebrows touching in an angry scowl. "Don't you want to keep playing your stupid little guitar?"

"Well, sure." He was curled into a ball on the couch, cuddling Rusty teddy bear-style. "And, he's not stupid."

"What if I told you you could do that forever? What if I told you you could go back and spend time with Stella? What if I told you you could relive that feeling, that 'Fourth of July in the guts' feeling, your book talked about, of playing to your first sold-out show?"

"I'd say, horseshit." Slowly, his body unraveled. "I don't know jack about science, but black holes sure as hell can't do all that."

"No, Claude, listen to me." She pinched his face and J. Claude's sleepy eyes flashed. This sudden rush of blood to the head brought his world into focus: the birds chirping in the trees, the smell of coffee brewing and maybe, at the right angle, Denny Dynasty being a woman. This so-called lady continued: "When Lloyd returns, we won't have much time, so everything has to go according to plan." Dynasty sat next to Claude and focused on his eyes until there was complete attention: "Our brother is going to build us a time machine. He just doesn't know it."

"Oh, sure. …whoops, I just invented time travel." J. Claude sat upright, shaking his head in disbelief. He strummed the first few notes of Stella. Claude's eyes were deep shades of red, the surrounding skin in sickly tones of purple. Hopelessness, Nashville's Shakespeare learned, had a weight to it—a heavy, crushing gravity. "I thought he was going to reverse the black hole or something?"

"That's his plan. But it's not reality. Just drop it and trust me."

"Oh, of course. My brother will just whip up a time machine. Then we all zip around the cosmos, visiting Jesus and stuff."

"Claude, don't be ridiculous," Dynasty's eyes turned sharp. He stood and paced the aisle. "Your chef is picking up sandwich supplies. I thought you knew."

"No, man, King of the Jews, that Jesus."

Dynasty stopped and delivered a gut-twisting look of pity. Claude was nine years old again and his sister was disappointed he wasn't smart enough to keep up at Monopoly, impatiently explaining rules once more. "Well, we don't exactly skip around outer space and, actually, we don't go back in time like tourists. I mean, yes, I'm from the future, I know how this all plays out. I know about what happens to Lloyd." Her lips cut off and she quickly grabbed the bubbling hot pot. "Coffee?"

"Wait, hold up," Claude said. His voice grew lively when he flipped on a cowboy hat. "So, tell me, Swami, why didn't Mom and Dad come back? For that matter, what were you all doing, going to those secret church meetings?"

Dynasty unrolled another sympathetic look and swiftly shattered Claude's belly with a cramp. "Mom and Dad. I'm sorry, brother, but Mom and Dad died. We were never in a church. Dad created all this. When we got close, he rented a shop in town. He quit his job at the University—"

"Wait, wait, wait," Claude laid Rusty at his side and stood. "Daddy was a meatpacker. He didn't work at the college."

"Damn it, Claude. You've been feeding that lie to reporters and fans so long you actually believe it. Dad was a physicist, like Lloyd. Always was. My god, what is wrong with you?"

"Nothing's wrong with me. I don't claim to be from the future and dress up like some gay cowboy. What's wrong with you?"

"Forget it, there's no time. We were never at some church. Mom and Dad and I were testing the machine. Believe me or not, but the cancer it gave our parents was real. Once we successfully went ahead a hundred years, they died. It took me decades to piece together his research and come back for you guys. And, yes, I am kind of lying to Lloyd. The diary is new. I bought it last week at Walgreens. But dunk it in water, stick it in the oven and, presto, it looks forty years old."

Claude made a look that matched his hopelessness.

"I had to. Lloyd wouldn't buy it otherwise. He's too logical."

"Sure."

"Look, I just want to take you with me. Show you how unbelievably important you've become." Dynasty blew on a mug of coffee.

"Keep talking." Claude ran massaging fingers around baggy eye skin. That familiar tug of sleep overcame him.

Her lips made reluctant stops and starts. "In the future, you are still famous. In fact, you're more popular. You finish your song about me and everyone loves it. The entire planet, actually. What's left after the black hole, at least—"

"Oh, good, genius, why don't you tell me the lyrics? I'm dying to know."

"I can't do that, Claude." She sipped coffee. "It'll come to you, you'll see."

"Sounds real reliable. Thanks. Go on, please," he extended a courteous hand, doused in sarcasm.

"Well, like I was saying, in the future The Ladies' Project is considered one of the cornerstones of artistic achievement. It's DaVinci, Van Gogh and Caruthers."

"Stupid DaVinci, what's he done for me lately?" J. Claude's possible sister made a face and it upset the country star. "Quit buttering my bread. Where's Lloyd while we're flying through time?"

Her lips fit together snug as hamburger buns. "Sacrifices are made." She offered a steamy coffee cup to Claude.

"Thanks, I need it," he grabbed the mug, blew across its top and gulped down half. "So we travel through time and stop this black hole?" J. Claude spat coffee grit into the carpet, reminding himself what a jerk Denny Dynasty had been in the past.

Claude was briefly swallowed by this black drainspout of a lie, but quickly regained common sense. This wasn't Denny's usual attack style, but seemed like a Dynasty-type way of screwing with Nashville's Shakespeare. "Time travel's a crock of shit."

"The hole gets close to Memphis. It practically stands on our doorstep and rings the buzzer before Lloyd solves the problem. This time travel, it also functions like a kick in the head to our little problem."

"You call getting sucked down some black straw a little problem?"

"Entering a collapsing star is not like getting sucked down a straw. Besides, you don't have to worry, you make it out of this mess just fine. Wait until you see the movie version. Tom Cruise's great grandson plays Lloyd. You're played by yourself, actually. It's all very exciting and touching. It won an Oscar."

"An Oscar, huh?" His head went a little airless, he drained the rest of the cup. "Never won one of those."

"Best Lighting, but still."

These words wrapped rubber bands around Claude's exhausted mind. And like a rubber band ball, they piled on top of one another until he couldn't untangle them. The majority of his heart knew time travel didn't make much sense and that Dynasty was just being a royal prick before everyone died. But another part of Claude's heart was relieved, it said his family was back together and, hell, he got to be immortal after all. But it all mixed into suffocating pressure, no matter which way was true.

"Alright, princess," Claude gave Dynasty a final stare-down. He hoped the Zygmut imposter would get weak at the knees just from its sharp appearance. "If you're really my sister, why are you Denny Dynasty? You could have been anyone. The president, a millionaire, a female country star, why invent a dude like Denny Dynasty?"

Possible Zygmut fixed her short hair, knocking the bangs from her brow. The stare down didn't even cause a flinch. "Two reasons: First, Denny is a lot of fun. If I'm going to risk life and limb going back in time, I figured I might as well have a ball. Second, haven't you ever heard the phrase, 'keep your friends close and your enemies closer?'"

"No, is that some sort of gay bar thing?"

"Look, you hate the president, you don't know any millionaires, you live on this bus for three-hundred-and-forty days a year, and I know you still miss Stella, so being a female singer wouldn't have helped me get near you. Plus, eww, kind of creepy. The only way to keep close tabs was to step on your turf as your worst nightmare. I'm sorry, Chubby. Before they died, Mom and Dad figured it was for your own good."

Claude looked up, opened his mouth to speak, but fizzled out. He jostled the guitar around, plinging strings and twisting tuners until all six harmonized. He looked up with a crooked mouth again, but quickly returned to the guitar for a few notes.

"Lies. I can't believe you were ever on Broadway, Denny. This is some Grade-A bad acting. There ain't no future traveling because my Mom and Dad and sister were in a cult. You don't even have your story straight."

"Chub, it wasn't a cult. Your imagination is getting the better of you. This is how history plays out. We help our brother and he saves everyone. You and I go forward a hundred years. You're famous. I didn't want to spoil it, but you bring Stella."

"Don't you dare say another word."

"It's the truth."

"I'll make a note of that." His voice was a frustrated growl. "I need some air."

"I knew you would," she said with a smiling face on the verge of smugness.

"Stop it, or else."

He didn't give Dynasty an opportunity to answer, slamming the door and squeezing Rusty's neck tight.

For nearly an hour, the confused country singer waded through the brush and weeds surrounding his old home. Occasionally, he made a lap through the house, running a sentimental finger along disintegrated wallpaper.

Resting his tired body on the back porch, strumming Rusty and whispering a melody, J. Claude let the shuffling sway of papery weeds act as a rhythm section. It reminded Caruthers of times when his drummer got jazzy after drinking too much bourbon, playing the snare with brushes.

He inhaled deep grassy fragrances and shivered. The weather was growing cool.

J. Claude's mind wasn't on chords and notes, though. He frequently closed those sourly tired eyes and let the morning sunshine coat his face. That magic comfort of sunbathing slowed his nervous heart and it soothed his anxiety. The world was soft and polite, like that 1977 summer, holding Stella in bed as the bus swayed down the highway.

A spark of anxiety returned as J. Claude recalled his talk with Dynasty. Was Claude's exhaustion getting the best of him, maybe just imagining all this?

Caruthers didn't know, but his heart claimed none of the options sounded all that seaworthy. "What does the truth even matter?" he asked the waving weeds, hopping up from the porch. "Whether it's a lie or not, one way or the other, I'm still going to die." His boots tightrope-walked down a small dirt vein running across the backyard, between the weeds. "Old age, cancer, stalkers, black holes—something'll get you, Claude."

Caruthers' brain and heart were cooperating like one of those two-man volleyball teams he'd seen on television. The duo was unraveling this rubber band ball when the country troubadour tripped. Claude's blue-jeaned knees dug into the dust and his toe throbbed. Rusty flew through the air and landed with an open chord twang.

"Son of a bitch," Claude's tense mouth shouted. If the toe wasn't broken, it was surely messed up bad enough for a doctor.

The sharp pain reminded him of that horrible day spent in a Clarksdale, Mississippi jail. The previous night, a fat, sweaty club owner said they didn't draw enough of a crowd to pay J. Claude and the band for their services. Claude saw the lancing grin across the owner's lips and knew this was another cheap shakedown. The club was packed and the future Nashvillian Shakespeare aimed to get the truth. So J. Claude Caruthers kicked the businessman in the face with that same foot. It throbbed mean, just like in the backyard.

This memory brought tears to Claude's eyes and, on his hands and knees, the salty solution slapped into the dirt. This kicking incident was long before Stella came into Claude's life.

There was no smiling under the neon beer lights of that Clarksdale juke joint. The owner was spread across cheap pine floorboards with blood leaking from his mouth. Initially, Claude figured the man was dead. At that moment, the singer realized knowing the truth isn't much help when the odds are stacked against you.

While endorphins and testosterone pulled the levers in Claude's head, inflicting pain on that cheapskate and teaching him a lesson was a logical conclusion. When the nuclear reactor in his brain melted down and his boot sliced through the barroom smoke and into the owner's jaw, J. Claude wanted to go back in time and stop himself.

He still wasn't getting paid. That club owner wasn't going to learn a damn thing. And, finally, J. Claude was on the receiving end of the bouncers' wrath, not to mention a lengthy court battle. The truth was, the truth never helped a damn thing.

The owner happened to be the brother of Mississippi's governor. This meant the heaviest legal hammer imaginable came down on the young troubadour to the tune of Attempted Murder. J. Claude, unable to afford help beyond a public defender, stared down a very realistic ten-to-twenty years in prison. His career, he assumed, was over.

But a day before the trial, the juke joint owner offered to settle out of court. It was a ridiculous compromise that would probably lead Claude back to jail, but he jumped at the opportunity. J. Claude turned over ninety-percent of his income until the club owner's settlement of fifteen million dollars was met. Around that time, J. Claude had a regional hit in the Delta and his earning potential was vastly overrated by the prosecuting attorney. It was not unlike blackmailing lawnmower commercial actors, assuming they were wealthy movie stars.

J. Claude jumped at the chance for freedom. Soon after, Claude got the brilliant idea to sing a song about every girl under the sun. While it was absent from the pages of *Nashville's Shakespeare*, Claude saw audiences light up and thought it would be a way to quickly pay off his debt. Those smiles soon grew narcotic. Over the past few years the singer realized the smiles would stop after Zygmut, which led to his original plan to commit suicide after its completion.

Money began pouring in, but the music industry being the music industry, J. Claude Caruthers saw about a dime of every eight-dollar album sold throughout the seventies and most of the eighties. Ninety-percent of those dimes went down to Clarksdale until recently. Claude's fifteen-million dollar debt was paid off a few years ago, but the singer still felt trapped. Starting the Caruthers' Kids Foundation helped a little, but the tiny singer knew he was a husk.

In his childhood backyard, with only his guitar watching, tears made a small pit of mud. The rhythm section of weeds kept shaking and the cooling breeze kept swirling.

"Even if you do go into the future, you'll still die, Claude," he said through a clogged throat.

Claude's body said: Why try? Quit. He considered lying in the weeds and letting Lloyd save the day. His mind replayed that Clarksdale face-kick a dozen times.

But in a heartbeat, he quickly shot up.

"Dynasty's full of shit," he whispered. "If I could travel back in time, wouldn't I have already gone back to stop myself from kicking that fat bastard club owner in the teeth?" Claude decided that probably would have been the first stop on his time travel itinerary. "There ain't no time travel. There ain't no Zygmut."

His fist hammered dry trail dirt and split apart the skin. That sleepless body ached. His mind was as far away from composing music as it had ever been.

And zap, like it was penciled into a calendar, melody interrupted J. Claude's little breakdown.

J. Claude's best song ideas always came at the most inopportune moments. Tongue-Twisting Tanya was composed during the dry heaves of a nasty flu in 1991. *Footloose, fancy free and Brittney* was tattooed to the singer's mind during Stella's funeral. And now, on the cusp of collapsing from exhaustion and dying from whatever that is, a decent melody and a sketchy set of lyrics scrolled through Claude's brain like closing film credits.

He shook his head, embarrassed about those slogans. "Why Try When You Can Quit?" "The Oyster is your World," "That's the Way the Crumble Cookies." They were just some ditzy political slogans used to medicate himself. They meant nothing and kept him from ultimately finishing that song. It was so easy to keep your own boot on your own throat. He didn't need outside help.

Claude rose. "Dying can go kiss my ass, Rusty, you know it? Legacies and legends, shit," he slurred that word as if it were carved from rotten fruit. "I always figured it'd be Kenny Rogers who killed me, not some science experiment." A deep mental focus paused the singer, the weeds and willows brushed over his ruddy cheeks. Claude wondered if the black hole was Lloyd's way of getting revenge for losing that hand. If it was, then he was ready to face death because life was now in such a clear focus. "There's only been two things I ever enjoyed in life, old buddy," with a bum toe he hobbled toward his guitar and lifted the six stringer. Rusty was scratched and covered in dust, but didn't look much filthier than normal. "Loving Stella and writing songs. I can't think of anything better than dying doing both those things."

His bloody knuckles formed chords and his sore throat began an ode to his sister.

TWENTY-TWO

"Club sandwiches are a whole hell of a lot like life. You chew on that for a while an' tell me I'm not right."
    -J. Claude Caruthers, *Nashville's Shakespeare*

Along the roadside, in front of a green barn advertising Rothrock Hog Farm, Memphis' morning wrapped colder and colder around them. This brutal change destroyed Lloyd's allergies like socks lodged down a throat.

A nauseous manure stink hummed from the barn.

But there wasn't much room for socks in Lloyd's neck, because something had been shimmying up his vocal chords since the barbecue restaurant. This tingle, this warm push was somehow brighter and more powerful than even those beautiful moments with Veronique.

Lloyd let Jesus drive the car and squeezed into the back seat after they left the parking lot, meat smoker in tow. Among the random coils of wire and electronic guts, he held Judy's hand.

Jesus rubbed the gnarled meat shank like a girlfriend's leg until the car shuddered and squealed and eventually jerked to a stop. They just passed the Memphis city limits, fully down a desolate stretch of road. Jesus called it the worst possible place for this stupid piece of junk to break down.

Lloyd tried diagnosing his simultaneously tight and queasy stomach. Would Einstein or Hawking understand? Were they ever in love?

"How's the tire coming?" he called to Jesus.

"It ain't good," Jesus stood from the wheel well and wiped a handkerchief over his face. "Axle's shot. Even if I replaced the tire, we wouldn't move an inch."

"Oh well," the physicist said. "That's the way it goes, I suppose."

"Hey, check it out," Jesus walked toward the long Rothrock Hog Farm barn. "Organic Bacon, Hams and Chitterlings. I got to check this out."

Lloyd's attention didn't linger on the chef or the car for long as he snugged hand and nub on Judy's hips. Her eyes peered down and focused on his, foreheads touching, noses nuzzling. "This is insane," he thought. "You've never moved this fast, Lloyd. Good god, did you just think about what she'd look like in a wedding dress? Snap out of it. Where did this come from?"

Judy's body grew rigid in Lloyd's hands. "We need to build this machine. You have to fix this problem."

Normally, Lloyd would have grown another dozen ulcers and let the world squeeze tight until he suffered the way he had for the past fifty-two years. Instead, with this bleachy fluid of love rushing through his veins, cleaning out the black negativity, the physicist sighed with a charming grin.

"If I'm meant to save the world, it'll happen," he gave a shrug. "If I'm not, I won't. But until then, I don't want to think about what's lurking out there. Let's just enjoy the moment, because that's something I'm terrible at doing."

A screeching patchwork of dark birds filled the sky, briefly making the blue atmosphere inky before their racket and flaps disappeared.

"Lloyd," her brows formed two steeples above dark brown eyes. She pulled him in confessionally close, "I…me too. It's…I don't want it to end, but you can't talk like that. You're the only one who can help. And I, for one, want us to have plenty of time on Earth," she kissed his forehead. "After you fix this mess." Judy mule-kicked the car with her heel.

The enormity of her words crept through that psychic wall Lloyd spent decades building. Like a condemned basement, doubt and pressure leaked back into his life. The sock in his throat was scratchy thick wool now.

A headache appeared and Lloyd's mouth opened to explain when a phone rang from inside Judy's purse. She leaned through the car window with a confused look.

Lloyd watched the slender woman dig for the call and a glistening, candy-coated peace returned. "That's her father," he thought. "She'll be so happy to hear his voice." The physicist forgot about allergies, his three heroes and the anxiety flooding that mental basement. He sat and fell backward across the dusty brown pavement. His eyes sealed shut.

The tall green treetops and their papery leaves impersonated a choir of rattlesnakes. Despite the rapidly cooling air, the astrophysicist was overcome with heat. A kerosene glow ran from his stomach to his chest.

"That was Denny Dynasty." Judy's disappointed face quickly matched Lloyd's. "He's coming to get us."

"Oh," Lloyd sat up. "I'm sorry. I thought that was a much more important call."

Judy's eyebrows built those steeples again. Her voice cut violently across the air: "Lloyd, that was about the most important call the world's ever known. Quit lying down like there's nothing to worry about."

He stood, but wasn't sure why. He wanted Judy to soak up that happiness as death caught them between its jaws and gave the lovers a final squeeze.

"For god's sake, you can fix all this and you're getting a sun tan?"

"I wasn't, actually. It's too cold. I was just thinking that you only start appreciating life once you're as good as dead." The scientist brushed red Tennessee dirt from his pants. "I'll shoot you straight and don't take this the wrong way, but I'm not worried if we're going to work as a couple. I'm just enjoying these excellent first moments of, you know, of," he gulped, "you know, whatever this is."

"You sound like your brother and his ridiculous sandwich fetish."

"Maybe I do. The world is a great place right now. But I never thought that until I met you."

"Well congratulations, you want me to put a flower in my hair?" she was into a spin, just as confused as Lloyd, but letting it fuel her temper. She easily slid into her old role with J. Claude. "Yes, quit. Great. This bullshit runs deeper in your gene pool than baldness. I swear."

The hog barn stink erased itself. The cool air numbed. Those rattlesnake trees shut up, too, as Lloyd's eyes grew enormous and his teeth clacked.

"But, personally, I'm not ready to die." Judy stood tall and looked back at the farm. "Jesus isn't ready to die, either."

"Yeah, man, I got a sandwich to make." The chef called and slammed the barn's door. He held a plastic bag saturated with swirls of raw pink and white flesh. "The place was empty, so I left five bucks on the table. I don't think they'll mind. This is some top notch bacon. Check out this marbling."

Judy held a hand toward Jesus. "Great, yes, thanks for the update." She returned her attention to the astrophysicist. "Help us unload all the stuff from this car and just don't talk, okay?"

"Okay." His voice was broken. No matter what distance he traveled, Lloyd couldn't escape science. It was always waiting around the corner with a baseball bat, foaming around the teeth, ready to crush Lloyd's happiness.

Minutes of silence passed as the elements from Zygumt's diary were unloaded and laid across the road. Jesus handled his sandwich ingredients like newborn babies. He proudly cradled fresh bacon under his arm.

The broken car was all but abandoned as Judy's most tender voice danced with the shuffling tree sounds. "So, how does all this save us exactly?"

He sifted through the tangles of wire and the random piles of junk, looking focused. In reality, the astrophysicist was hoping to avoid answering.

"Well," Lloyd flexed his good hand until a knuckle crackled. "There's no guarantee. Probably less than a guarantee, whatever that is. But, I mean, in theory this equation seems airtight, knowing what I already know about particle collisions, etcetera."

"That diary makes sense?"

"Absolutely," he was lighting up, fitting back into a comfortable rut of scientific babble talk. "It's all just thermodynamics. Not unlike, I suppose, how tornadoes form. A warm front butts against a cold front and you get a twister. Well, the theory here is that you take an incredibly cold proton and an incredibly hot one and bash them together at subatomic speeds. This creates a balance to our little problem. A molecular jetstream that pushes away instead of pulling in. Ideally, they'll envelope one another and level out." A slickness of sweat built on the rear of Lloyd's neck. His nerves were acting brutal. He looked up at the violent trees coughing in the wind. Their dance didn't settle his uncertainty. "Ideally."

Denny honked the bus horn from down the road. When he pulled next to the random scatter of gear and people, the window rolled down. "You ready to live on forever, Lloyd?"

All the physics talk, coupled with forgotten urges for immortality, brought Lloyd back to his Hadron Collider self. He was ready to take ten paces and fire against his life's work. Maybe Judy had a point, if the first hour of love felt this good, who wouldn't want another few decades worth?

It also didn't hurt that whatever tiny scraps remained of his macho side thought saving the planet would be a cool way to smooth things over with the still-irritated Judy.

Loading the gear into the bus, Dynasty pulled Lloyd aside, but broadcast his secret in a booming voice. "Doctor Lloyd, it's time you and I were completely honest with one another. Before you save the planet and all."

His hazy eyes focused on Dynasty. "I'm sorry, what do you mean?"

"You know those letters you've been getting from Zygmut?"

"Supposedly, Zygmut. I don't have any proof. Claude seems think—"

"Well, what if I had a way of clarifying all that?"

TWENTY-THREE

"If a song can't be written in twenty minutes, it ain't worth writing."
    -J. Claude Caruthers, *Nashville's Shakespeare*[5]

Every strum nearly shattered Rusty. His normally sturdy neck was a wobbly spaghetti noodle, his bridge was carved from peanut brittle and the strings latched on by a fingernail. For Rusty, J. Claude's fall in the backyard was the equivalent of a senior citizen tumbling down stairs.

Nashville's Shakespeare hadn't noticed.

J. Claude's guitar playing found a focus previously vacant for decades. Intensity and purpose filled his picking and chording until shivers flew down the guitar's backside. "God, I feel like an asshole," Rusty thought, remembering his eagerness to run off with another musician only a few hours earlier. Guilty heat burned through the instrument, imagining those tasteless fantasies. "J. Claude's not so bad. The truth is we just got lazy, we both got comfortable."

Rusty realized how badly he missed that comfort while locked in an airtight guitar case. His brief preview of life inside a coffin glamorized his outlook on practically everything. Grass was greener, J. Claude's playing sounded better. Heck, his boss even smelled better than usual and Rusty was positive Caruthers didn't know the meaning of deodorant.

He was humbly prepared to grace that big stage in the sky,

---

5 Again, upon further research, the author discovered this was said by Hank Williams Sr.

but wasn't exactly thrilled. Rusty didn't know if there was a Guitar Heaven or a Guitar Hell. Though, he was pretty sure any Guitar Hell would look something like a coffee house open mic night.

He'd played shows with guitars in religious bands and they said you had to be a good six stringer every day and stay out of trouble and do right to avoid damnation. J. Claude once shared a bill with a heavy metal Creedence Clearwater Revival cover band called Bayou Hazard. They had a custom-built, penta-gram-shaped guitar who told Rusty that Hell wasn't as bad as people made it sound. He claimed the acoustics down there were excellent. Once, Rusty even met an agnostic guitar with another cover band: John Cougar Summercamp. Its version of death sounded a lot like being locked in a guitar case—all eternity and empty darkness.

Rusty never followed a particular belief system. He always figured someday he'd either be hanging in a pawn shop or a country music museum and would seek out god then. But death was sneaking up on Rusty and the guitar was wandering around with its pants down.

"No, no, no," J. Claude said, leaning against a tree in front of the house. "That don't sound right." He plucked some strings and sang a few tense lines. His voice wasn't as golden and confident as normal. Caruthers and the melody blindly groped one another. Luckily, his sour voice evaporated into the stiff wind. Rusty wondered if the black hole was causing this breeze, sucking oxygen into its depths.

Since his fall, the grungy guitar focused incredible amounts of energy just staying in tune. He understood the staggering pain J. Claude's insomnia brought. Rusty assumed it felt a lot like falling apart at the joints and screws. But the guitar loved hearing where Caruthers was taking him.

"What rhymes with Zygmut?" Claude said and flipped Rusty over so his backside faced the sun. "Let's just make sure nobody's hanging around," Claude quickly glanced over a shoulder. "I swear, this song's going to kill me. What in the hell rhymes with Zygmut?"

The coast was clear, the purple bus was still gone, so J. Claude pulled out a pen and a paper scrap. "Holy cow," Rusty thought as the point dug into his back and scratched across the paper. "He's writing. Claude can write." The guitar waited to make sure Caruthers wasn't just doodling a picture, but Rusty knew the swoop and structure of honest-to-goodness letters. The guitar filled with enthusiasm at the prospect of a miracle. "This never would have happened without me," Rusty thought. "Through my suffering, beautiful things occurred." It was obvious to Rusty that, because he pulled himself together in a painful time of darkness, J. Claude was struck by a lightning bolt of literacy. Some subliminal force, he decided, was guiding them.

Rusty soaked up the weak daylight and pride, feeling Claude make notes and curse under his breath. "Come on, man," Claude said. "You've rhymed a million words before. You just got one more to go. Pull it together. Come on."

This intimate moment ended when the bus crunched down a long gravel path. J. Claude quickly stuffed the paper into a pocket.

The bus unloaded and Rusty sensed a playful bounce in J. Claude's steps: "Good news, y'all. Zygmut's practically in the can." He walked closer to the bus. "Don't start crying or nothing, Denny. I'm sure you'll write a real nice tune about kissing dudes named Frank or something." The group met this information with silence. "Anyway, there's just one little snag I can't work through. But it's close, it's damn close. Feels good."

"Hey Claude," Jesus stuck his head from the bus window. "I'm making a sandwich. You wait until you taste this baby. It'll be the best club anyone's ever eaten."

The singer waved a hand of encouragement at the chef.

"You're writing a song at a time like this?" Denny's voice was some androgynous yowl. "The fate of the world is on the line and you're plucking that stupid guitar?"

"Fate of the world? You sure love the drama, huh? Denny, get real. I figured out what's happening. You can't fool J. Claude Caruthers, little Miss Gloom and Doom."

"Claude, Denny," Judy yelled and slid between them. She was a veteran peacemaker. "Let's give Lloyd all the support we can. We don't have much time. The radio says Nashville is gone. We probably only have a few more hours."

"Then, Judy." Claude gave his publicist's hand a tender squeeze, "enjoy that time."

"Not now, Claude."

"Don't sweat and stress over dumb experiments. Don't punish yourself. You're too good of a person…"

"Quite a compliment, but I think your brother needs help carrying things. Someone able-bodied as yourself should realize that."

His voice perked up, "Look at me. My legacy's nothing but bullshit and I don't care. I just want to go out on a high note. You should, too."

"I'd rather not go out, period."

"I'm gonna start right now. Something I've been meaning to mention for a while, but, well, pride being a son-of-a-bitch and all." His face took on a rosy hue. "Look, I never said this at the time, never said it in court, but I should have. I'm sorry for shooting you in the arm."

There was a long supply of motionlessness in the trees, with the wind and between the singer and his publicist.

Judy slapped her boss and the surprise made J. Claude Caruthers drop his most prized possession. Rusty fell into the gravel with a familiar open note clonk. "Selfish," she hissed.

"Come on, let's set up the computers," Lloyd said in what Rusty assumed was a sneer. He had a difficult time focusing, his body's wood and wire were dangling toes over some cliff. Had Rusty been born an airplane, he would have been coughing fumes and helplessly dive bombing toward Earth.

"Hey, listen to me," Rusty heard his boss say. "It's pointless. We're all dead. We've all been inching closer to it our whole lives. Well, death's got our address and casket measurements. So let's get along. There is no fixing this shit, so we should all just chill out. There is no time machine. Denny's just a royal asshole."

"Wait, wait, wait," Lloyd said.

"J. Claude, don't you dare let jealousy get in the way." Judy was nearly to tears. "Your brother is the most important man on Earth. Try to understand you aren't the center of the universe." Judy grabbed the nearby physicist and laid a strong kiss.

"Come on, cheer up." J. Claude laughed. "The center of the universe is some enormous black hole."

Rusty closed his eyes and staggered toward some blinding light down a tunnel.

Nashville's Shakespeare took a few steps toward them. "Hey, wait, you two are kissing now?"

"Yes," she said with her chin held up, dignified and a small curl of a smile forming.

"Wait a second," Lloyd spoke up, his good hand chopped through the air. "Hey, wait just a damn second."

"Well that's fantastic," J. Claude said. "Enjoy love while you can." He clutched Judy's small hands with crusty, calloused fingers. "Hey, remember when I got that online preacher's license and married Barney Thackery and Paul Lutz?"

"Excuse me," Lloyd's voice grew loud and raw.

"I could marry you and Lloyd right now." J. Claude's green eyes danced with possibilities. "It'd be beautiful. Oh man, that class is turning into the best fifty bucks I ever spent."

"Wait!" Lloyd sliced a raised hand for attention. "Time machine?"

"Man, brother, you believe everything Old Man Dynasty says, huh?"

"Claude, it's our sister." Lloyd's wrinkles tensed into a face lift. "Denny is Zygmut, she told me on the bus."

"Wow, Dynasty is cooking up a cow's asshole and calling it steak." He gave his twin a nice slap on the shoulder. "Looks like you got A-1 on your chin, Lloyd. Let me tell you how it really is."

Rusty giggled as the white light around him grew warmer.

TWENTY-FOUR

"It's all about Rusty, man. If everyone in the world had a Rusty, it'd be a much safer place, you know?"
  -J. Claude Caruthers, *Nashville's Shakespeare*

Horrible silence filled the minutes after J. Claude explained "how it really was." But the unexpected destruction following this speech zip-tied the group's vocal cords.

This shocked tension was smashed and stomped upon by Nashville's Shakespeare. "You're fired," the enormous meat smoker heard the man in the cowboy hat say. The little guy seemed happy when they pulled up, but since that guitar split in half, this J. Claude seemed much quieter. "No, wait, Judy, I take it back."

"What are you talking about?" Everyone but the cowboy moved toward the Smoker. It was nice being so important. The plump guy with a ponytail was weaving cables in and out of the Smoker's hull. "For the last time, give us a hand." Oddly, this scientist set three framed photos on the Smoker's rack.

The Smoker admired its view. Some crummy house was off in the distance, down the driveway a bit. Dense trees surrounded the group, limbs bending severe from wind.

"Put yourself in my shoes. Your sworn enemy has your twin brother convinced he's not only your sister, but that he knows how to stop that thing. All the while, you see right thought this shit and nobody cares."

"Quit it."

"It's like I'm buying a one-wheeled motorcycle and you're telling me it's a hotrod."

"Claude, not now," Judy's voice was a bear discovering wounded hikers in the woods.

"Then, right before this shit sandwich world comes to an end, I decide maybe I can make someone happy by marrying them. But no, they'd rather fiddle with a barbecue grill and die alone and unloved."

"Claude, I liked you better as a pervert," she snapped. "Forget about marriage and let your brother focus."

"It's cool that you don't want to get married. I overreacted," the little cowboy said. "But why stomp on Rusty?"

"To prove a point."

"That guitar was more like a brother to me than my own brother."

"Nice, thank you," the chunky guy said. "I'm not even here."

"But that's just me being stupid. I see it now. Rusty was just a thing, wasn't he? Things don't matter when you're dead. Things won't keep you from dying." The man's hand bobbed into his jeans pocket and pulled out a wrinkled pack of cigarettes. "You see what I'm saying?" The pack crinkled, a lighter flickered and the man soon blew grey smoke into the wind. He hobbled toward them as if a toe were broken. "None of this matters. Building some time machine isn't going to help. Do you think you're some Egyptian pharaoh, think you can take it with you? Man, I used to be like you, obsessed with living forever. But it's all crap, brother." Claude's face shifted, it was something reluctantly confident. "Let me guess, you want people to wait in the heat for hours just to walk past your casket and pay their respects when you die. Something royal like that."

"M—" the stutter came without a thought. "Maybe."

"Good luck, that'll do you a lot of good." He turned and muttered, walking off: "Knowing my luck, sons of bitches will probably be lined up past Clarksdale to rub my coffin. Probably come in wagons and busses and time machines."

The ponytail man stopped fiddling inside the Smoker like some tease. After decades of sitting in the back lot of Jim Neely's, surrounded by barbed wire, the modified propane tank was out in the world and doing something besides cooking meat. The Smoker liked the idea he was supposed to save the planet.

"Why does he keep saying that?" the chubby guy said. "He keeps saying it's a time machine. Do I have to keep explaining that is impossible?"

"Just ignore it, baby brother," Denny Dynasty said. "We need you to finish this project and create a white hole. It's the only way to save us and your legacy. It's amazing how people think of Lloyd Caruthers in the future. Families hang portraits of you in their living rooms like they used to with George Washington and Martin Luther King.

"He keeps calling this a time machine." The man's thick fingers began shaking.

"Claude's an idiot. He's always been an idiot. Remember that time when we were little, he got his head stuck in the banister?"

"The third time?"

"That's my point. Our brother, god love him, is a moron."

That moron carried the mangled guts of an acoustic guitar in his arms. His facial muscles yanked and stretched in ways that held tears back.

"Okay," the man said. "Now what?"

A small diary was opened and the two crowded around. "It's simple, see here where I talk about charging the vacuum tubes with positive ions—"

The moron interrupted them. "Okay, time traveler," his voice was lined with broken glass. "Where's your time machine? How'd you get back here? Tell everyone how you decided to return as a man-loving country superstar. That's a realistic story. Maybe Lloyd would like to hear it, too. I think we could all take a break and listen. Or are you too scared my brother will see you're using him for this sick joke?"

The Smoker had a hard time focusing. These humans were shoving and pushing one another, screaming. The small group twisted and scrambled quickly.

But something stopped the ruckus.

And loudly.

J. Claude's cowboy hat flipped backward through the air when a crack of thunder rattled the Smoker's thick metal walls. A hazy cloud cleared and the Denny guy stood holding a shiny pistol. The moron was stiff, still clutching at the ruins of a guitar, but not bleeding. That cowboy hat, lying in the grass, was split apart at the hollow portion above the skull.

"That sounds familiar," Claude said.

"J. Claude, it's time you finally took that nap. Leave us alone and stop asking stupid questions." The thin man with pasted-on eyelashes clicked back the hammer. "Or I'll put you to sleep myself."

The singer breathed a few shallow lungs full and the neck of his guitar fell and dangled by a shiny metal wire. "Is that?" he stammered, "is that my gun?"

Meanwhile, the banging and rattling inside the Smoker continued. The young, pretty girl and the ponytail man weren't worried about gunfire. They rushed around. This was fine by the Smoker, all this action filled its grease-smeared heart with pride.

"I'll count to three, Claude," the man or woman with the gun said.

"You won't."

The Smoker was trying to pay attention, but there was suddenly a lot of action where its racks used to be. Computers were hooked up and wires attached and a lot of other confusing things it didn't understand.

"One…"

"Not a chance."

"Two…"

"You won't kill me if you really are Zygmut," the tiny cowboy said as guitar bits and splinters clacked to the ground. "You said I was famous in the future. So if you are my sister and not Denny Dynasty, you'll let me live." Claude's face was confident and carved.

"Why would Denny even want to kill you?" The Judy woman said. "Quit screwing around before someone gets hurt."

The cowboy descended to something shy and wincing. "I may have held a knife to his throat."

"I could care less about this," Dynasty pointed to a shallow red slice on his neck. "You are getting in Lloyd's way and in the way of history." He stepped closer and from the Smoker's perspective, the man with the gun aimed it right between the cowboy's eyes. "Now, I'll start over and count to three. You can count, right?"

"Shit," the ponytail man muttered, lost in his world of physics.

"Which one is it? Are you Denny or Zygmut? I'm ready for either. So pull that trigger, Denny, or answer my question, Ziggy."

The sky and clouds had dimmed to murky gray streaks above the trees. The wind twisted the home's ancient weather vane in squeaky circles. The tinkering stopped within the Smoker and this noise drove it nuts. The cooker hated hearing unlubricated metal-on-metal.

The man with the ponytail asked the young woman something, but the Smoker couldn't hear with all the commotion.

"J. Claude Caruthers," Dynasty said. "You are the world's premiere idiot." Dynasty kept the gun trained at his head.

"I've been going back and forth on knowing the truth. I think I want your side of this mess before we die. Because we are going to die. Your whole story is a load of crap."

"Damn!" The ponytail's rage screeched through the clearing and made birds fly off. "We're missing a wire. One stupid wire." He slammed a hand painfully into the Smoker's side.

Lloyd's furious fist made a gong of the Smoker. Waves of sound filled the charcoal dark air.

The crowd watched, open-mouthed, as the scientist stomped around the gravel. He cursed and squeezed the dirty rubber hand on his side.

Lloyd ran eyes up and down over his brother. "Claude, you want to see if Ziggy's lying?" There was a beat of pause, but not enough for Nashville's Shakespeare to answer. "Give me one of those guitar strings and let me finish wiring this up. We'll see who's a liar."

TWENTY-FIVE

"Why try when you can quit?"
   -J. Claude Caruthers, *Nashville's Shakespeare*

Tempers cooled with the temperature. As heart rates returned to normal, the twins held a private meeting fifty yards from the smoker. Denny, Judy and Jesus watched at a distance, unable to hear the Caruthers boys.

Weird vibrations pebbled off Lloyd. This invisible anger shifted Claude's feet uncomfortably, wanting to talk about anything but the obvious.

"This weather's getting weird," J. Claude told his brother, kicking his head back to watch a flock of birds. It was the tenth cluster he'd seen that hour. A huge dark swarm of flapping wings and piercing cries. Those fowl packs all headed west. J. Claude assumed they were running from the black hole. "I mean the birds and the wind and just how cold it is. Man, Lloyd, you're shivering."

"I'm fine," he said, bending over and picking up Claude's destroyed cowboy hat, offering it to its owner.

"No, thanks. I think that puppy's seen better days."

Lloyd shrugged and tossed it on his own head.

"You look good, brother. Maybe you could be my stunt double. Or better yet, you could go on tour as me. We could cover opposite coasts. How's your singing voice these days? That dude, Gallagher, the comedian with the watermelons, did the same thing in the 70s with his brother."

162

"Quit changing the subject," Lloyd blew warm breath into a cupped hand. "I need that guitar string. Our lives are hanging from a little stretch of wire. Don't be selfish." The astrophysicist hugged himself and rubbed upper arms. "Don't be typical J. Claude."

A strange gagging reaction tightened the singer's throat. "Things must be getting desperate in Lloyd's mind," J. Claude thought. "He's always been the nice one. For him to be a prick, his brain must be worn down worse than mine." Claude tried to blame his brother, but Lloyd's accusations felt truer and truer. J. Claude had been looking out for number one and cutting down the weeds around him for decades.

"Since Stella died I haven't had much reason to think about everybody else," he coughed once to fill the silence.

"It's time, Claude. Please." His brother was desperate and eyeing the shards of guitar with the lust of a shore leave sailor.

"But I'm so close. I've got this melody in my head. I can almost touch this song. The end of my project, Lloyd." He shuffled random pieces of wood and wire. "You ever have that feeling, like your work is never done? I'm close finally. I just need to put Rusty back together. A little tape, some staples and—"

Another fat cloud of birds bucked the turbulent overhead breeze.

"This pile of trash can't be more important than what I'm doing." Lloyd clutched his brother's shoulders with real and rubber hands, looking deep into Nashville's most bloodshot eyes. "Please, just give me the string."

"Quit jabbering about fate of the planet, crap. Denny's fooled you, man. He's just getting back at me. There is no emergency exit. We're all toast."

"Not everything is about you, Claude. What does it take to understand that," Lloyd poked his finger through the charred bullet blast atop the hat. "Now I'm walking away with that wire, one way or another."

"Why is it that I'm always the idiot? I'm wrong about Zygmut. I'm wrong about this dumb smoker. Why can't I ever be right?"

"You're doing it again. It's not about you. It's about helping. Making sacrifices. You don't think I want to curl into a ball and die right now? But I can't because there's a job to do."

"It's not real. This thing. You're not going to create some reverse hole. You're not even going to make a time machine. Denny Dynasty is the world's biggest asshole. Period. He's doing this just to get one last laugh." Claude clutched the ruined instrument tighter and stepped backward. "Me, I'm not interested in the last laugh or the truth anymore. I just want to finish my song and die smiling."

Lloyd's hands fell from J. Claude's shoulders. He winced and massaged his nub, which had turned a cold shade of pink beneath aged rubber.

"What's the matter?" J. Claude said, lips forming something impatient.

"This stupid hand. My brain says there's something here," he groaned low and weak. "But it's clearly impossible."

"I know what you mean."

"Look." He checked to make sure Judy was out of earshot. "I know this sounds stupid. I know it doesn't seem possible that a smoker and a bunch of wires could do anything. And the whole Denny Dynsaty/Zygmut thing, too. But my entire life was spent judging what is scientifically possible and impossible. And you know what?"

Claude didn't answer, pulling guitar scraps tighter to his chest and clamping a chin over the top. A foggy curl of breath met the rapidly cooling air.

The wind whipped Lloyd's ponytail loose from beneath the hat. He tucked the strands under the brim until it looked like his hair was shorter than Claude's. "I don't care. I want to believe there are things beyond our control. I tried determining how the universe began with the most advanced scientific experiment in history and look what happened. You said it yourself, physics has never made anyone happy."

"Oh, now I'm not such an idiot."

"Scientific thought's brought me nothing but pain. So I figure I'll give faith a shot. It's already made me a lot happier." He checked over his shoulder. "So if I die, you know, oh well. I tried."

Claude nodded in Judy's direction, she looked sweet and lonely standing by the bus, red hair twisting in a hundred directions. "So you and Judy are an item. When'd this happen?"

"I wasn't looking for it, but it feels nice, right?" He smirked and gently rubbed eyes. "It's narcotic. I'd be happy living the last few hours over again for the rest of my life."

A familiar boulder hopped onto J. Claude's shoulders. He'd been pushing this impossible rock uphill for years with The Ladies' Project, now convincing his twin brother to give up looked equally hopeless. Claude's eyes whipped up, his mouth released an exhausted breath: "Why try when you can quit?"

"What?"

"Nothing. Something I used to say."

Lloyd looked back at the others. J. Claude watched the publicist give a gentle wave and a smile to his brother. The image cut through the howling wind and the blowing house debris.

He didn't know why Lloyd was fighting until that moment. J. Claude recognized that look. It was a smile and wave like Stella would give. Whenever butterflies attacked his belly before a big concert or she bit her fingernails prior to an impressive jump, the other would give a quick wave and a smile. A small, goofy, unnecessary gesture that removed the tea pot from the fire. Love and faith broadcast in Technicolor 3-D.

Judy shared that with Lloyd. The singer filled with an odd warmth that sheltered the frosty wind.

Soon, the breeze was silenced by a wooden clank and thin, metallic pling of broken guitar crashing into gravel. Nashville's

Shakespeare held his hands out to his sides.

"Do me a favor, though," J. Claude said, humbly.

Lloyd crouched and sifted through the wreckage. "Absolutely, anything."

Normally, all those years on stage and his starring role in the short-lived 80s detective show, *Caruthers for Hire: Backwoods Sleuth*, gave Claude a knack for timing. But his instincts were off and J. Claude hadn't actually planned a speech. "At first, I thought I'd say something cheeseball, like 'just be happy for the rest of your life, whether it was eight minutes or eighty years.' But that's a load of crap. I almost said you better treat Judy like a lady, or else. But I know you will. So I got one simple favor."

"Anything, Claude, I'm serious," Lloyd pulled a string from the pile as if finding a gardener snake. He tipped back the hat and showed J. Claude a set of caring, sweet eyes.

"You been to a lot of schools. Taken a shitload of boring classes, I bet. Maybe you can tell me something that's been bugging me for a while now," his tired eyes looked into Lloyd's.

"I'll try, Claude," he stopped eyeing the silver wire and focused on Nashville's Shakespeare.

"You're going to think I'm an idiot again. But I can't write a song that doesn't rhyme. Can't do it, absolutely impossible. So, I'm wondering if you can think of anything that rhymes with Zygmut?"

TWENTY-SIX

"Only songs I like that don't rhyme are church songs. And, hell, most of them rhyme too, right?"
  -J. Claude Caruthers, *Nashville's Shakespeare*

Lloyd's watch said it was just after lunch, but dusk arrived much earlier than usual. Since his face was shoved into the smoker, the physicist hadn't noticed until he looked for the man claiming to be his sister.

"Okay, I've double and triple checked the wiring, the connections, the alignment," Lloyd said, wiping soot from cheeks, a grey smear across the chin. "Just like your diary says." He picked up the savory smells of wood smoke and pork fat from the cooker.

He looked to Zygmut, still dressed as Denny Dynasty and wearing a set of pinched lips, deep in thought. With nose pointed to the tree tops, she released a long-held breath: "Check it again."

"Again?" Judy said, wrinkles of worry across her face matched. "Aren't we cutting things close?"

Zygmut slowly shook her head. The wind whipped hunks of heavily gelled hair against her face. "No. This is how things are supposed to happen."

"You've got to be kidding."

"It's okay. Just go for a walk, relax," Lloyd held Judy close and gave her a brief forehead kiss, smelling the apple and soapy clean hair. "See if you can track down Claude, I'm worried, I haven't seen him for an hour."

Some murky part of Lloyd's brain felt he and Claude were working together on this contraption. Much the same way he praised the underlings at the Hadron for their contributions to the big picture, the white hole was lost without wrapping that piece of wire, this piece of J. Claude Caruthers' life, into the mechanical works.

A problem arose regarding the wire's lack of insulation, but Lloyd solved that issue by trimming and carving a portion of his rubber hand to wrap around the cable. He briefly admired the mangled work, considering it the best thing he and his brother had done together since constructing a boyhood tree house.

Lloyd's satisfaction died quickly. Claude gave a gift to help the physicist and Lloyd wanted to return the favor. J. Claude Caruthers' life hinged on a single word. All the fame and money and immortality in Claude's back pocket weren't enough to shield this unfinished bitterness. It spread and swallowed up any relief the scientist had left.

This wasn't some Jack and Jill went up the hill-type rhyme. The man's scientifically sharp mind drew a blank.

It wasn't blank for long, though. Lloyd couldn't stop the image of backing away with that string, watching Claude shiver and turn pale. It stung the scientific twin. He had to focus on this makeshift atom smasher, but poor Claude's face crept into dashing equation lines running through his head.

Walking away with that guitar string wasn't a victory moment. It reminded Lloyd that, like science, life always felt hollow. There was always so much left undone. Science was closing doors, and life was still being a son-of-a-bitch. Nothing was ever final. "Claude and I," he thought, "are suckers for bottomless projects."

Checking his connections once more with blackened fingertips, a clot of regret jammed into Lloyd's concentration—times when he picked on Claude and called him dumb as children, terrorizing him to the point where he was actually illiterate. A sinkhole opened within the physicist. Lloyd regretted his sixteen-year-old self blaming Claude for blowing off his hand. Lloyd regretted pushing his only brother so far away. The scientist regretted going to Yale and MIT and Oxford. If he'd have skipped just one of them and come home to be a librarian, like he truly desired, he never would have discovered the pain and competition and boulder-pushing of the scientific life.

A stinging sniff of old smoke caught the breeze and found the astrophysicist. The birds, black and brown wings struggling against the invisible current, chattered above.

Lloyd took comfort realizing those wrong turns led him to Judy. Unlike the rest of his life, she wasn't a suffocating, collapsing bubble of worry. The past few hours with her had all been fresh air and open spaces of possibility. It was, Lloyd rolled his eyes with teeth spreading into a smile, just like a quote he recently learned. When killing time last night, he finally cracked open *Nashville's Shakespeare* and found a passage that rang loud now. His moments with Judy were the first sip of beer or the first bite of a sandwich.

But dreamy memories of Judy didn't last either. The regret punched into Lloyd's stomach with the force of a license plate press. That word was pounded out in hollow letters he couldn't ignore.

Regret.

He mumbled it, eyes following multicolored wires to motherboards and barbecue racks. He closed those eyes and leaned close to the photos of Einstein, Oppenheimer and Hawking. "This pile of junk doesn't look like it could save the planet, does it?"

Their images held steady. This recent faith-based version of Lloyd hoped for a voice to tickle his ear. He wanted Einstein or Oppenheimer to admit this was a waste. It became clear these men weren't enemies. There was no competition among geniuses. They were some kind of imaginary clubhouse. But, like in life, friends don't always have the answers. "This thing looks like something Claude and I would have slapped together after the tree house. God, I miss those days. I should have kept a journal or something. Why didn't I hold those memories tighter?" His chest hummed as he relived those scraps. That regret hammered deeper. "Those connections are all I'll have when—"

Lloyd's knees caved and grew weak when an idea struck.

"Where's J. Claude?" he yelled, pulling himself from the smoker's belly.

"What does it matter?" Zygmut said, still watching the skies as they turned a smoker's shade of brown and grey. "We don't have time. You need to start the countdown soon."

"I need to help him, just real quick." Lloyd started half-skipping, half-running around the gravel. His smile was an enormous shape it hadn't formed since childhood.

"Stop, stop, this isn't part of the plan," Zygmut screamed, focusing her attention on Lloyd's backside as the scientist ran toward the bus. "I know how everything works and this isn't it."

The physicist popped the bus door open: "Claude, Claude," he hollered into the cabin, running back to the bedroom.

"Silence," Jesus screamed, leaning over the kitchen counter, paying close attention. "It's almost finished. My masterpiece. This is going to give your stomach a boner."

Lloyd stopped, huffing for breath. His foot landed directly on top of a bedroom floor sandwich. The room was empty, the bed a tangle of purple sheets. "Have you seen my brother?"

"No, man. I've been a little busy. But tell him he needs to be the first to try this." Jesus held a slide ruler across the bread. A dark pink blush of ham, rust-colored bacon and sharp green lettuce spilled from its sides.

"I'll let him know," Lloyd said, dashing out the door with childish zeal.

Lloyd ran through a tornado of dead leaves and into the weeds circling the house, latching his brother's hat to his head with a free hand. Dark green and yellow thickets brushed against his skin with barbwire viciousness. He leapt up the porch and crashed open the front door. "Claude, hey Claude," he screamed.

Lloyd's shoes slowed their pace, pounding through the Cape Cod. Feet scraped along the old crumbles of sheetrock and decades of dirt along the dusk-lit floor. He kept one sweaty hand against a wall for guidance. "Claude, are you in here?"

The dying light outlined a cloud of breath in the icy air.

Silence made Lloyd nervous. Brief flickers of J. Claude's depression and the possibility of suicide brushed against his mind with the violence of those barbwire thickets and weeds.

Out the back door, he howled for his twin again.

Life, he decided, is nothing more than those silly connections. Eating and talking and meeting new people and trying new things were happiness. And really, what else did he need?

Lloyd wanted one last connection with his twin. The perfect one hung to a life preserver in his mind.

Guitar guts were strung around the back patio. Lloyd collected them and spotted a hunk of dark wooden neck lying partway down a dirt path. A canopy of weeds haunched over the fretboard. He ducked and shuffled down the trail, picking up tiny scraps of Rusty. An ulcer of worry grew with each step.

"Claude?" Lloyd's voice was desperate and scared.

The rustling path wound forever. Each step ached like an hour. Lloyd's head darted in all directions searching for a sign of life, but chances felt slim.

Weeds whipped his face, blinding the scientist until he nearly tripped over his brother's body, curled in the middle of the path.

The cold atmosphere sunk through Lloyd's bones with arthritic brutality. The world was a silent bubble for a moment.

It was ready to collapse one final time onto the scientist. "I'm sorry," Lloyd's guilty conscience said. "I wasn't fast enough."

Lloyd dropped a knee amongst a gagging fever of tears. J. Claude was motionless and Lloyd knew he'd helped this man kill himself.

Without warning, sound returned to the world. Noise crashed back in the form of a snore.

J. Claude Caruthers sounded like a garbage disposal. The breathing was fast—sleeping in overdrive, making up for lost time.

Earlier, Judy told Lloyd how long it had been since J. Claude had a good night's sleep. She explained his miserable, staggering final tour around America, trying to write that song. It sounded absolutely awful to Lloyd.

The singer's tiny limbs were pink and shivering.

Lloyd swallowed a fist of tears. He leaned over his brother, stroking coarse, curly hair. He slipped off a jacket and blanketed his brother. When he was tucked in snug, Lloyd bent down to the singer's ear and whispered. "I've got your rhyme, buddy. Don't worry about a thing."

"There you are," Zygmut said as Lloyd emerged from the brush. The physicist had to squint in the darkness. "Get over here now. We don't have much time." She cocked her head to the sky. The clouds were pockmarked tails, swishing in one direction.

"Sorry, I had to tell J. Claude something," he grinned and walked as if maybe the apocalypse wasn't playing solitaire just beyond the tree line.

Zygmut slapped the diary into Lloyd's palms. A fat paper bookmark caught a gust, flapping with the intensity of a sail.

"The combination is written down, it's your time to shine." Her eyes were forceful and intense.

"Ziggy, why me?" His lips twisted into a rose of confusion.

"Fate, Lloyd. It's always been you."

"But," walking down the driveway, the smoker came into Lloyd's focus. "If you know all this stuff, why aren't you pulling the trigger? Why do you need to wait for me? Unless this is some sort of trap, like Claude said."

"Very funny. Lloyd, you created this mess and I'm giving you a chance to fix it. Everything rests with these keystrokes. If you really want me to be the hero and live on forever—" she clawed at the book.

Something defensive jerked Lloyd's hand toward the charcoal sky. Zygmut didn't even try to reach. The threat raised his blood pressure in a way nothing had since battling the Orange Team for first dibs at the Hadron Collider. He didn't have time to give his sister botulism and knew it wasn't necessary.

"Okay, okay, okay," he said, still raising the diary high. "Relax." Lloyd brought the directions to his chest and waited until that vicious gleam disappeared from Zygmut's eyes. "Just punch a few keys, right? I guess now we'll see if Claude's hunch was correct."

"It should be that easy. I mean, I haven't read the diary in years." She gently rubbed his stiff shoulders. "Trust me."

Judy returned from her walk, arms wrapped around her chest. Deep red hair lifted and flapped in the wind with unpredictable jerks.

Jesus stepped from the bus holding a silver platter with a tall stack of meat, vegetables and bread. "Where is he? Did you find him?"

"Yeah, but—" Lloyd met Judy and swallowed her into his arms.

"Where is he? J. Claude is going to love this." Jesus held the platter to Lloyd's face. It didn't look like anything special to the physicist.

"He's sleeping, Jesus. It can wait."

"Wait, hell. I didn't stop you when you were playing with the barbecue grill."

"That's not the same."

"That's your little finale, I get that. This is mine," he sniffed at the sandwich below his nose. Jesus' face stiffened with pride.

Those words dropped Lloyd's excitement into a dark pit. He was sick of seeing so many disappointed faces. "Okay," he sighed and pulled Judy's warmth in tighter. "Around the back of the house. But let him get a little more shuteye, okay?"

"Whatever you say, ace," the chef carefully walked away, balancing the tray.

Lloyd made a tender look at Judy. She returned it with nervous, bulging eyes.

"It's time, it's time," Zygmut's hand made some gentle pressure on the center of Lloyd's back. "Hurry, hurry."

Lloyd walked to a glowing black and green computer screen atop the closed smoker. Figures and words splashed across in some homemade programming he'd never encountered back at his lab. He read the diary instructions by monitor light. The physicist carefully pressed a series of keys, frequently going back between the diary and the keyboard to make sure the combination was perfect.

Three framed photos were piled at his feet. Lloyd's electricity couldn't have been matched by Einstein or Hawking. They never actually did anything. They were probably more miserable than Lloyd ever was, just theorizing all damn day.

But Oppenheimer had a connection. He probably shared that same red hot poker of nerves in his bowels, too, before the first explosion. But Lloyd felt he had the upper hand since his work was finally causing good. The father of the atom bomb was never celebrated as a hero. His legacy was calloused and ugly. When he died, all he had left where those little connections of memorable meals and people. Lloyd knew that's all he'd have too, but old familiar thoughts stabbed into his heart. Visions of his reputation resembling something speckled with jewels or carved from gold dominated him. These thoughts were too powerful to ignore.

With only the ENTER key left to press, Lloyd paid extra attention to his stump. Sharp nerves shattered a bottle and rubbed the glass into the phantom hand much like that Hadron moment of truth. However, back in Switzerland he was alone and pushed the button with a cold empty chest—pressed purely for himself. This time, he glanced over at Judy and a wet heat filled his body, knowing their future rested upon this moment. A first bite was great, but a lifetime was better.

"Will we be safe so close to this?" Lloyd asked. He hadn't had time to contemplate what would actually happen with a white hole. He quickly speculated the electromagnetic forces could blow them into Arkansas.

Or not.

"Lloyd, please!" Zygmut snapped, massaging her hands and staring into the starless dark sky. "Just do your job. Hurry."

Judy and Lloyd shared a queasy shrug. The love of the physicist's life closed her eyes and bit her lip.

Lloyd surprised himself. He pressed the ENTER key without hesitation.

He surprised himself again by repeating that infamous Oppenheimer quote.

He jogged backward, waiting for a brilliant light or explosion.

Nothing happened. The wind whistled constantly and the faint call of overhead birds meshed with the throbbing in his ears.

The smoker began humming loud. Clanging and plinging sounded over the rushing wind, but still nothing happened.

Leaves tore buzz saw paths between Lloyd and the machine. He wrapped an arm around Judy's shoulder. They hugged tight and the physicist's mind wandered.

Just as Lloyd prepared to call over to his sister, worried something didn't work, there was movement. The smoker hiccupped and grumbled, like an elderly preacher standing on the pulpit, clearing his throat before a final sermon. The machine ended its homily with a dull metal thump like someone was beating the lid with a hammer.

And then nothing again.

The sky was shaded like a deep bruise. Strange winter cold swept in from the West. The blood still beat a drum skin between Lloyd's ears. His breaths came in short jabs, too frightened to relax. But still, nothing happened.

Oppenheimer's words sounded so microscopic now. So ridiculous. "I have become death, the shatterer of worlds."

Silent minutes evolved and dozens of leaves turned to paper bullets. Shivering, he hollered over the wind: "Zygmut, what did I do wrong?"

Equations began filtering through his mind. He mentally checked his work and searched for the error.

Ziggy's boots crunched through the gravel. When she neared, the smiling face of Denny Dynasty—the same one Lloyd once saw hanging on a giant poster outside a rainbow-themed bar in Geneva—came into his sphere of vision.

"Congratulations, brother. You did it." Zygmut said, shaking Lloyd and Judy's hands. The joy in her face scraped against Lloyd's frightened nerves.

"Did you see the same thing I did?" He released the handshake to rub his stump.

"That's it, that's all there is to it. You just saved everyone. Everyone not already dead. Trust me, I wish it was more dramatic, but that's the big show. You just wait and see. You'll be impressed."

"But nothing feels different," Judy said. "Look around us."

"It's alright. You'll see. Lloyd is now officially immortal." Zygmut leaned into Judy. "This is the right time to give our hero a kiss."

Lloyd's brow pinched his eyelids. An emotional double helix twisted through his body. One pole was excited to hear he saved the world, and would be fondly remembered. But the other pole felt tricked and worse, felt J. Claude was right. These two emotions wrapped incestuously around one another.

A strange noise popped through the air. Hard, rhythmic steps.

"Congratulations," Judy was tense and her voice was flat. She sensed Lloyd's doubt and couldn't bring herself to comfort him.

The sound of sledgehammers mashing gravel rose until the intensity sliced through the harsh wind. Judy turned and squinted into the darkness.

Lloyd watched Judy, nuzzled her cheek and kissed it. He held on to that warmth, but the physicist couldn't stall the words forever. "Whatever happens, we're together. Whenever science closes a door, life kicks in the windows."

The sound evolved into a horse's clip-clop. The three turned to face the woods giving birth to these strange sounds.

From the tree line, a man in black riding gear with a thick white beard appeared atop a dark horse.

"Kenny," Zygmut's voice was laced with nervous energy.

The sleek thoroughbred stepped closer and Lloyd recognized the man. Kenny Rogers was the biggest star in country until Claude came on the scene. Rogers looked remarkably good for someone his age.

"What the Hell is going on out here?" Rogers asked. "What are you and J. Claude Caruthers doing together?"

"Kenny," Zygmut grasped the man's boot. "It's not what it looks like. This isn't even J. Claude, it's his twin brother. He just saved the world. You should thank him."

Rogers sneered. "What was all that business last night, taking that guitar and that gun?"

"I needed it. It's a long story, Kenny. But you have to believe me." Desperation soaked each word. Lloyd's leg twitched, it worried him to see his sister so upset.

"Well, I came out here to die, like I promised. Got a stable a few miles to the East. Came to die like those proud elephants in Africa. Now, I don't know what you're all up to and I don't give a damn. We're all dead."

"No, it's not true," Lloyd spoke up.

"We are, J. Claude. It's a scientific fact." Rogers tilted his head and leaned into the darkness. "You look good without a mustache, by the way."

"I'm not J. Claude," the physicist felt Judy's fingernails deep into his arm. "Oh, this hat, I see. No, I'm his brother. My name's Lloyd. Pleased to meet you." He removed the hat, and his hair flowed out in a dramatic waterfall. "I really enjoyed *The Gambler* movies. The fourth one was the best, though. In my opinion—"

"Nice try, that's a classy wig. Looks better than your boyfriend, Dynasty's." Kenny removed a silver gun from his coat. "Remember this? I bought it at an auction. It was your second-favorite gun.

"Denny, we are going to talk about the one you stole from me. But for now, since I came out here to die alone, there's no reason I can't take J. Claude with me."

"No, you don't understand." Judy yelled. "Mister Rogers, please. This man is a hero…" her voice trailed, "I think."

"See, we don't know if this experiment I tried worked or not."

"Don't care," Rogers clicked back the pistol's hammer. "Nobody breaks my brother's jaw and kicks my mama. You sick, twisted son-of-a-bitch."

Rogers snapped his eyes shut. The crowd looked up, not moving, not wanting to disturb the country legend.

"That's good. I think you should take a deep breath, Ken." Dynasty's voice slit like a blade. Zygmut removed an identical silver pistol.

The group stood with nervous blood warming their cheeks. Dynasty pointing a gun at Rogers. Kenny Rogers pointing his gun at Lloyd. Judy cinched tight against her man.

TWENTY-SEVEN

"Rule number one, baby, you gotta end an album on a high note. You don't do that, ain't nobody gonna spin it a second time."

    -J. Claude Caruthers, *Nashville's Shakespeare*

"Bacon? Is that bacon?" J. Claude thought in a womb of darkness. His mind was sparking to life, gaining a little momentum. This, he assumed, is what being inside a black hole was like.

"Eh," he thought, "this ain't so bad. What was Lloyd so scared of? Being dead is warm, dry and smells like bacon. I should have killed myself years ago."

Nashville's Shakespeare enjoyed eternity for a few seconds longer.

Slowly, a rush of cold prickled his senses. A gentle voice filtered into this charming darkness. In an erratic jerk, the singer realized he was not finally dead, but actually sleeping. After insomniac weeks, finally, sleep! Unfortunately, someone was interrupting it.

"Try it, man," the voice urged. "Come on, Claude, you'll love it."

J. Claude rode a rollercoaster drop of waking. He was disoriented, not recognizing the darkness and weeds all around him. His eyes snapped open and closed until they focused. Jesus knelt in the dirt. Something shimmered in his hand, swaying like liquid moonlight.

"That a boy," Jesus was excited, patting the country star on the leg. The air was rich with savory bacon.

"Hey, man," Claude coughed. "Good to see you too, buddy. What's going on? Was I finally sleeping?"

"Yeah, boss. Looks like you conked out right here in the dirt. But that's not important. Feast your eyes on this."

The liquid moonlight turned out to be a silver platter. J. Claude recognized the silhouette of a sandwich. He groped the darkness until fingers met the bread's spongy skin.

"Now? Jesus, you out of your mind? Aren't you the dude who got all pissed at me for wanting to eat at funky hours? Now, we're about to die and you fix me a sandwich?"

"I had to. It's the best club ever made. It'd probably cost a hundred bucks at a deli. Imported ham from Spain, organic bacon..." he stopped and his voice grew low and warm, "I know that stuff doesn't matter to you. Just taste it, give it that first bite. It's my life's work."

The chef's eyes sparkled in the disappearing light. J. Claude was horrible at telling, but Jesus might have been crying.

Claude didn't know how to thank the chef. For years, he was the only person on this planet who wasn't asking something of J. Claude Caruthers. Jesus wasn't using the singer to get ahead. Hell, the chef never once even asked Claude to belt out a complimentary tune. Never.

Claude wanted to tell Jesus what a valuable friend he'd been. But hefty internal filters held the singer back. Several false starts ramped up in his mind, but each felt phony and forced and the kind of thing that would embarrass his favorite cook.

One plan caught on, though, and Claude prepared to give Jesus the biggest thank you imaginable. He squeezed the bread between his hands and dug in.

Claude's jaw worked slowly. His tongue darted around, groping textures and flavors. His brain started playing tricks, his head filled with something like carbonation bubbles. His mouth was coated in a zingy sensation of salty, sweet and meaty. "It tastes like the first bite all over again. Every bite is like the first."

An instinct led Claude to the sandwich for another bite, and another and another. He chewed and returned, chewed and returned, until there was only a jagged hunk left. A spurt of pricey French mayonnaise leaked to the ground.

"Hot damn, man," J. Claude said, wiping his forehead. "That was delicious. What the hell's gotten into you?"

"Really? You think so?"

"You ever seen me eat a whole sandwich?"

A proud bob took over Jesus' head, neck and shoulders.

"Here man, I'm stuffed." J. Claude extended a hand. "You eat the last bite. I insist."

"No, really. That was just for you."

"Please, it'd make me happy."

There was a moment of staring. Claude admiring the work and his chef too nervous to move.

Jesus eventually grabbed the sandwich nub and popped it into his mouth. His eyes closed and he chewed with erotic speed. A slow, powerful nod built up steam.

Claude opened his mouth to speak, but was interrupted by a fierce noise.

Years of firearm ownership told him it was the unmistakable discharge of a gun. "That sounds like one of mine," he cocked an ear toward the driveway. "One of my silver Colts..."

A swarm of nothing followed this disruptive shot. All hushed breeze and weeds.

Jesus and J. Claude stood. The tips of the brush met their shoulders. They traded suspicious glances.

"Well," J. Claude spoke quiet and careful. "I guess we should go check that out."

The pair crept down the path until the weeds cleared and they faced the backside of the dilapidated Caruthers homestead. J. Claude paused, debating whether to go through the house or around when Jesus smacked his arm.

The chef stared into the eggplant dark sky, pointing.

A lone bird, delivering a sharp hello, flew overhead. J. Claude focused for a moment, getting his bearings straight. For the first time all day, he saw something flapping from west to east—toward where the black hole should be.

ABOUT THE AUTHOR

Patrick Wensink does not teach creative writing at some school everybody's heard of. He was never awarded a Master's degree in anything. He got a Bachelor's degree...but just barely. He has never won any awards, which is a shame, because that would look good right here. His mom was probably very embarrassed that his first book was called *Sex Dungeon for Sale!* (Eraserhead Press, 2009). Look for his next Lazy Fascist book, *Broken Piano for President,* in October 2011.

Patrick lives in Louisville, KY. You can discover all things Wentastic at www.patrickwensink.com.

Bizarro books

CATALOG	SPRING 2011

Bizarro Books publishes under the following imprints:

www.rawdogscreamingpress.com

www.eraserheadpress.com

www.afterbirthbooks.com

www.swallowdownpress.com

For all your Bizarro needs visit:

WWW.BIZARROCENTRAL.COM

Introduce yourselves to the bizarro fiction genre and all of its authors with the Bizarro Starter Kit series. Each volume features short novels and short stories by ten of the leading bizarro authors, designed to give you a perfect sampling of the genre for only $10.

BB-0X1
"The Bizarro Starter Kit"
(Orange)
Featuring D. Harlan Wilson, Carlton Mellick III, Jeremy Robert Johnson, Kevin L Donihe, Gina Ranalli, Andre Duza, Vincent W. Sakowski, Steve Beard, John Edward Lawson, and Bruce Taylor.
236 pages $10

BB-0X2
"The Bizarro Starter Kit"
(Blue)
Featuring Ray Fracalossy, Jeremy C. Shipp, Jordan Krall, Mykle Hansen, Andersen Prunty, Eckhard Gerdes, Bradley Sands, Steve Aylett, Christian TeBordo, and Tony Rauch. **244 pages $10**

BB-0X2
"The Bizarro Starter Kit"
(Purple)
Featuring Russell Edson, Athena Villaverde, David Agranoff, Matthew Revert, Andrew Goldfarb, Jeff Burk, Garrett Cook, Kris Saknussemm, Cody Goodfellow, and Cameron Pierce **264 pages $10**

BB-001 "The Kafka Effekt" D. Harlan Wilson - A collection of forty-four irreal short stories loosely written in the vein of Franz Kafka, with more than a pinch of William S. Burroughs sprinkled on top. **211 pages $14**

BB-002 "Satan Burger" Carlton Mellick III - The cult novel that put Carlton Mellick III on the map ... Six punks get jobs at a fast food restaurant owned by the devil in a city violently overpopulated by surreal alien cultures. **236 pages $14**

BB-003 "Some Things Are Better Left Unplugged" Vincent Sakwoski - Join The Man and his Nemesis, the obese tabby, for a nightmare roller coaster ride into this postmodern fantasy. **152 pages $10**

BB-004 "Shall We Gather At the Garden?" Kevin L Donihe - Donihe's Debut novel. Midgets take over the world, The Church of Lionel Richie vs. The Church of the Byrds, plant porn and more! **244 pages $14**

BB-005 "Razor Wire Pubic Hair" Carlton Mellick III - A genderless humandildo is purchased by a razor dominatrix and brought into her nightmarish world of bizarre sex and mutilation. **176 pages $11**

BB-006 "Stranger on the Loose" D. Harlan Wilson - The fiction of Wilson's 2nd collection is planted in the soil of normalcy, but what grows out of that soil is a dark, witty, otherworldly jungle... **228 pages $14**

BB-007 "The Baby Jesus Butt Plug" Carlton Mellick III - Using clones of the Baby Jesus for anal sex will be the hip sex fetish of the future. **92 pages $10**

BB-008 "Fishyfleshed" Carlton Mellick III - The world of the past is an illogical flatland lacking in dimension and color, a sick-scape of crispy squid people wandering the desert for no apparent reason. **260 pages $14**

BB-009 "Dead Bitch Army" Andre Duza - Step into a world filled with racist teenagers, cannibals, 100 warped Uncle Sams, automobiles with razor-sharp teeth, living graffiti, and a pissed-off zombie bitch out for revenge. **344 pages $16**

BB-010 "The Menstruating Mall" Carlton Mellick III - "The Breakfast Club meets Chopping Mall as directed by David Lynch." - Brian Keene **212 pages $12**

BB-011 "Angel Dust Apocalypse" Jeremy Robert Johnson - Methheads, man-made monsters, and murderous Neo-Nazis. "Seriously amazing short stories..." - Chuck Palahniuk, author of Fight Club **184 pages $11**

BB-012 "Ocean of Lard" Kevin L Donihe / Carlton Mellick III - A parody of those old Choose Your Own Adventure kid's books about some very odd pirates sailing on a sea made of animal fat. **176 pages $12**

BB-015 "Foop!" Chris Genoa - Strange happenings are going on at Dactyl, Inc, the world's first and only time travel tourism company.
"A surreal pie in the face!" - Christopher Moore **300 pages $14**

BB-020 "Punk Land" Carlton Mellick III - In the punk version of Heaven, the anarchist utopia is threatened by corporate fascism and only Goblin, Mortician's sperm, and a blue-mohawked female assassin named Shark Girl can stop them. **284 pages $15**

BB-021 "Pseudo-City" D. Harlan Wilson - Pseudo-City exposes what waits in the bathroom stall, under the manhole cover and in the corporate boardroom, all in a way that can only be described as mind-bogglingly irreal. **220 pages $16**

BB-023 "Sex and Death In Television Town" Carlton Mellick III - In the old west, a gang of hermaphrodite gunslingers take refuge from a demon plague in Telos: a town where its citizens have televisions instead of heads. **184 pages $12**

BB-027 "Siren Promised" Jeremy Robert Johnson & Alan M Clark - Nominated for the Bram Stoker Award. A potent mix of bad drugs, bad dreams, brutal bad guys, and surreal/incredible art by Alan M. Clark. **190 pages $13**

BB-030 "Grape City" Kevin L. Donihe - More Donihe-style comedic bizarro about a demon named Charles who is forced to work a minimum wage job on Earth after Hell goes out of business. **108 pages $10**

BB-031"Sea of the Patchwork Cats" Carlton Mellick III - A quiet dreamlike tale set in the ashes of the human race. For Mellick enthusiasts who also adore The Twilight Zone. **112 pages $10**

BB-032 "Extinction Journals" Jeremy Robert Johnson - An uncanny voyage across a newly nuclear America where one man must confront the problems associated with loneliness, insane dieties, radiation, love, and an ever-evolving cockroach suit with a mind of its own.   **104 pages $10**

BB-034 "The Greatest Fucking Moment in Sports" Kevin L. Donihe - In the tradition of the surreal anti-sitcom Get A Life comes a tale of triumph and agape love from the master of comedic bizarro.   **108 pages $10**

BB-035 "The Troublesome Amputee" John Edward Lawson - Disturbing verse from a man who truly believes nothing is sacred and intends to prove it. **104 pages $9**

BB-037 "The Haunted Vagina" Carlton Mellick III - It's difficult to love a woman whose vagina is a gateway to the world of the dead. **132 pages $10**

BB-042 "Teeth and Tongue Landscape" Carlton Mellick III - On a planet made out of meat, a socially-obsessive monophobic man tries to find his place amongst the strange creatures and communities that he comes across. **110 pages $10**

BB-043 "War Slut" Carlton Mellick III - Part "1984," part "Waiting for Godot," and part action horror video game adaptation of John Carpenter's "The Thing." **116 pages $10**

BB-045 "Dr. Identity" D. Harlan Wilson - Follow the Dystopian Duo on a killing spree of epic proportions through the irreal postcapitalist city of Bliptown where time ticks sideways, artificial Bug-Eyed Monsters punish citizens for consumer-capitalist lethargy, and ultraviolence is as essential as a daily multivitamin. **208 pages $15**

BB-047 "Sausagey Santa" Carlton Mellick III - A bizarro Christmas tale featuring Santa as a piratey mutant with a body made of sausages. 124 pages $10

BB-048 "Misadventures in a Thumbnail Universe" Vincent Sakowski - Dive deep into the surreal and satirical realms of neo-classical Blender Fiction, filled with television shoes and flesh-filled skies. **120 pages $10**

BB-049 "Vacation" Jeremy C. Shipp - Blueblood Bernard Johnson leaved his boring life behind to go on The Vacation, a year-long corporate sponsored odyssey. But instead of seeing the world, Bernard is captured by terrorists, becomes a key figure in secret drug wars, and, worse, doesn't once miss his secure American Dream. **160 pages $14**

BB-053 "Ballad of a Slow Poisoner" Andrew Goldfarb Millford Mutterwurst sat down on a Tuesday to take his afternoon tea, and made the unpleasant discovery that his elbows were becoming flatter. **128 pages $10**

BB-055 "Help! A Bear is Eating Me" Mykle Hansen - The bizarro, heartwarming, magical tale of poor planning, hubris and severe blood loss... **150 pages $11**

BB-056 "Piecemeal June" Jordan Krall - A man falls in love with a living sex doll, but with love comes danger when her creator comes after her with crab-squid assassins. **90 pages $9**

BB-058 **"The Overwhelming Urge" Andersen Prunty** - A collection of bizarro tales by Andersen Prunty. **150 pages $11**

BB-059 **"Adolf in Wonderland" Carlton Mellick III** - A dreamlike adventure that takes a young descendant of Adolf Hitler's design and sends him down the rabbit hole into a world of imperfection and disorder. **180 pages $11**

BB-061 **"Ultra Fuckers" Carlton Mellick III** - Absurdist suburban horror about a couple who enter an upper middle class gated community but can't find their way out. **108 pages $9**

BB-062 **"House of Houses" Kevin L. Donihe** - An odd man wants to marry his house. Unfortunately, all of the houses in the world collapse at the same time in the Great House Holocaust. Now he must travel to House Heaven to find his departed fiancee. **172 pages $11**

BB-064 **"Squid Pulp Blues" Jordan Krall** - In these three bizarro-noir novellas, the reader is thrown into a world of murderers, drugs made from squid parts, deformed gun-toting veterans, and a mischievous apocalyptic donkey. **204 pages $12**

BB-065 **"Jack and Mr. Grin" Andersen Prunty** - "When Mr. Grin calls you can hear a smile in his voice. Not a warm and friendly smile, but the kind that seizes your spine in fear. You don't need to pay your phone bill to hear it. That smile is in every line of Prunty's prose." - Tom Bradley. **208 pages $12**

BB-066 **"Cybernetrix" Carlton Mellick III** - What would you do if your normal everyday world was slowly mutating into the video game world from Tron? **212 pages $12**

BB-072 **"Zerostrata" Andersen Prunty** - Hansel Nothing lives in a tree house, suffers from memory loss, has a very eccentric family, and falls in love with a woman who runs naked through the woods every night. **144 pages $11**

BB-073 **"The Egg Man" Carlton Mellick III** - It is a world where humans reproduce like insects. Children are the property of corporations, and having an enormous ten-foot brain implanted into your skull is a grotesque sexual fetish. Mellick's industrial urban dystopia is one of his darkest and grittiest to date. **184 pages $11**

BB-074 **"Shark Hunting in Paradise Garden" Cameron Pierce** - A group of strange humanoid religious fanatics travel back in time to the Garden of Eden to discover it is invested with hundreds of giant flying maneating sharks. **150 pages $10**

BB-075 **"Apeshit" Carlton Mellick III** - Friday the 13th meets Visitor Q. Six hipster teens go to a cabin in the woods inhabited by a deformed killer. An incredibly fucked-up parody of B-horror movies with a bizarro slant. **192 pages $12**

BB-076 **"Fuckers of Everything on the Crazy Shitting Planet of the Vomit At smosphere" Mykle Hansen** - Three bizarro satires. Monster Cocks, Journey to the Center of Agnes Cuddlebottom, and Crazy Shitting Planet. **228 pages $12**

BB-077 **"The Kissing Bug" Daniel Scott Buck** - In the tradition of Roald Dahl, Tim Burton, and Edward Gorey, comes this bizarro anti-war children's story about a bohemian conenose kissing bug who falls in love with a human woman. **116 pages $10**

BB-078 **"MachoPoni" Lotus Rose** - It's My Little Pony... *Bizarro* style! A long time ago Poniworld was split in two. On one side of the Jagged Line is the Pastel Kingdom, a magical land of music, parties, and positivity. On the other side of the Jagged Line is Dark Kingdom inhabited by an army of undead ponies. **148 pages $11**

BB-079 **"The Faggiest Vampire" Carlton Mellick III** - A Roald Dahl-esque children's story about two faggy vampires who partake in a mustache competition to find out which one is truly the faggiest. **104 pages $10**

BB-080 **"Sky Tongues" Gina Ranalli** - The autobiography of Sky Tongues, the biracial hermaphrodite actress with tongues for fingers. Follow her strange life story as she rises from freak to fame. **204 pages $12**

BB-081 **"Washer Mouth" Kevin L. Donihe** - A washing machine becomes human and pursues his dream of meeting his favorite soap opera star. **244 pages $11**

BB-082 **"Shatnerquake" Jeff Burk** - All of the characters ever played by William Shatner are suddenly sucked into our world. Their mission: hunt down and destroy the real William Shatner. **100 pages $10**

BB-083 **"The Cannibals of Candyland" Carlton Mellick III** - There exists a race of cannibals that are made of candy. They live in an underground world made out of candy. One man has dedicated his life to killing them all. **170 pages $11**

BB-084 **"Slub Glub in the Weird World of the Weeping Willows"** **Andrew Goldfarb** - The charming tale of a blue glob named Slub Glub who helps the weeping willows whose tears are flooding the earth. There are also hyenas, ghosts, and a voodoo priest **100 pages $10**

BB-085 **"Super Fetus" Adam Pepper** - Try to abort this fetus and he'll kick your ass! **104 pages $10**

BB-086 **"Fistful of Feet" Jordan Krall** - A bizarro tribute to spaghetti westerns, featuring Cthulhu-worshipping Indians, a woman with four feet, a crazed gunman who is obsessed with sucking on candy, Syphilis-ridden mutants, sexually transmitted tattoos, and a house devoted to the freakiest fetishes. **228 pages $12**

BB-087 **"Ass Goblins of Auschwitz" Cameron Pierce** - It's Monty Python meets Nazi exploitation in a surreal nightmare as can only be imagined by Bizarro author Cameron Pierce. **104 pages $10**

BB-088 **"Silent Weapons for Quiet Wars" Cody Goodfellow** - "This is high-end psychological surrealist horror meets bottom-feeding low-life crime in a techno-thrilling science fiction world full of Lovecraft and magic..." -John Skipp **212 pages $12**

BB-089 **"Warrior Wolf Women of the Wasteland" Carlton Mellick III**
Road Warrior Werewolves versus McDonaldland Mutants...post-apocalyptic fiction has
never been quite like this. **316 pages $13**

BB-090 **"Cursed" Jeremy C Shipp** - The story of a group of characters who
believe they are cursed and attempt to figure out who cursed them and why. A tale of
stylish absurdism and suspenseful horror. **218 pages $15**

BB-091 **"Super Giant Monster Time" Jeff Burk** - A tribute to choose your
own adventures and Godzilla movies. Will you escape the giant monsters that are rampaging
the fuck out of your city and shit? Or will you join the mob of alien-controlled punk rockers
causing chaos in the streets? What happens next depends on you. **188 pages $12**

BB-092 **"Perfect Union" Cody Goodfellow** - "Cronenberg's THE FLY on a
grand scale: human/insect gene-spliced body horror, where the human hive politics are as
shocking as the gore." -John Skipp. **272 pages $13**

BB-093 **"Sunset with a Beard" Carlton Mellick III** - 14 stories of surreal
science fiction. **200 pages $12**

BB-094 **"My Fake War" Andersen Prunty** - The absurd tale of an unlikely soldier
forced to fight a war that, quite possibly, does not exist. It's Rambo meets Waiting for Godot in
this subversive satire of American values and the scope of the human imagination. **128 pages $11**

BB-095 **"Lost in Cat Brain Land" Cameron Pierce** - Sad stories from a surreal world. A fascist mustache, the ghost of Franz Kafka, a desert inside a dead cat. Primor-
dial entities mourn the death of their child. The desperate serve tea to mysterious creatures.
A hopeless romantic falls in love with a pterodactyl. And much more. **152 pages $11**

BB-096 **"The Kobold Wizard's Dildo of Enlightenment +2" Carlton
Mellick III** - A Dungeons and Dragons parody about a group of people who learn they
are only made up characters in an AD&D campaign and must find a way to resist their
nerdy teenaged players and retarded dungeon master in order to survive. **232 pages $12**

BB-097 "My Heart Said No, but the Camera Crew Said Yes!" Bradley Sands - A collection of short stories that are crammed with the delightfully odd and the scurrilously silly. **140 pages $13**

BB-098 "A Hundred Horrible Sorrows of Ogner Stump" Andrew Goldfarb - Goldfarb's acclaimed comic series. A magical and weird journey into the horrors of everyday life. **164 pages $11**

BB-099 "Pickled Apocalypse of Pancake Island" Cameron Pierce A demented fairy tale about a pickle, a pancake, and the apocalypse. **102 pages $8**

BB-100 "Slag Attack" Andersen Prunty - Slag Attack features four visceral, noir stories about the living, crawling apocalypse. A slag is what survivors are calling the slug-like maggots raining from the sky, burrowing inside people, and hollowing out their flesh and their sanity. **148 pages $11**

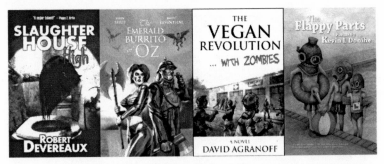

BB-101 "Slaughterhouse High" Robert Devereaux - A place where schools are built with secret passageways, rebellious teens get zippers installed in their mouths and genitals, and once a year, on that special night, one couple is slaughtered and the bits of their bodies are kept as souvenirs. **304 pages $13**

BB-102 "The Emerald Burrito of Oz" John Skipp & Marc Levinthal OZ IS REAL! Magic is real! The gate is really in Kansas! And America is finally allowing Earth tourists to visit this weird-ass, mysterious land. But when Gene of Los Angeles heads off for summer vacation in the Emerald City, little does he know that a war is brewing...a war that could destroy both worlds. **280 pages $13**

BB-103 "The Vegan Revolution... with Zombies" David Agranoff When there's no more meat in hell, the vegans will walk the earth. **160 pages $11**

BB-104 "The Flappy Parts" Kevin L Donihe - Poems about bunnies, LSD, and police abuse. You know, things that matter. 132 **pages $11**

BB-105 **"Sorry I Ruined Your Orgy" Bradley Sands** - Bizarro humorist
Bradley Sands returns with one of the strangest, most hilarious collections of the year.
130 pages $11

BB-106 **"Mr. Magic Realism" Bruce Taylor** - Like Golden Age science fiction comics written by Freud, *Mr. Magic Realism* is a strange, insightful adventure that spans the furthest reaches of the galaxy, exploring the hidden caverns in the hearts and minds of men, women, aliens, and biomechanical cats. **152 pages $11**

BB-107 **"Zombies and Shit" Carlton Mellick III** - "Battle Royale" meets "Return of the Living Dead." Mellick's bizarro tribute to the zombie genre. **308 pages $13**

BB-108 **"The Cannibal's Guide to Ethical Living" Mykle Hansen** - Over a five star French meal of fine wine, organic vegetables and human flesh, a lunatic delivers a witty, chilling, disturbingly sane argument in favor of eating the rich.. **184 pages $11**

BB-109 **"Starfish Girl" Athena Villaverde** - In a post-apocalyptic underwater dome society, a girl with a starfish growing from her head and an assassin with sea anenome hair are on the run from a gang of mutant fish men. **160 pages $11**

BB-110 **"Lick Your Neighbor" Chris Genoa** - Mutant ninjas, a talking whale, kung fu masters, maniacal pilgrims, and an alcoholic clown populate Chris Genoa's surreal, darkly comical and unnerving reimagining of the first Thanksgiving. **303 pages $13**

BB-111 **"Night of the Assholes" Kevin L. Donihe** - A plague of assholes is infecting the countryside. Normal everyday people are transforming into jerks, snobs, dicks, and douchebags. And they all have only one purpose: to make your life a living hell.. **192 pages $11**

BB-112 **"Jimmy Plush, Teddy Bear Detective" Garrett Cook** - Hardboiled cases of a private detective trapped within a teddy bear body. **180 pages $11**

9 781936 383511